Wild Hearts

LINDSAY DETWILER

HOT TREE
PUBLISHING

For information, contact the publisher, Hot Tree Publishing.

www.hottreepublishig.com

Editing: Hot Tree Editing

Cover Designer: Claire Smith

Formatting: RMGraphX

ISBN: 978-1-925655-48-3

10 9 8 7 6 5 4 3 2 1

More From Lindsay

THEN COMES LOVE SERIES

Then Comes Love

Where Love Went

Where Love Went (Holiday Special)

LINES IN THE SAND SERIES

Inked Hearts

Wild Hearts

STANDALONES

Remember When

To Say Goodbye

Who We Were

All of You

Still Us

*To my husband, for always being
my motivation to keep going;
to my best friend, Jamie Lynch,
for inspiring me to live more adventurously;
and to Ocean City,
my favorite beach to visit since childhood.*

Chapter One

"That's it, that's it, *that's it*!" I scream at the top of my lungs, the fiendish creature's squawk the final straw. I don't care if I'm wearing the scandalously thin pajamas Avery bought me as a birthday gift. I don't care that my mascara is smudged from being up all night, or that I haven't shaved my legs in days.

I don't care because that maniacal parrot and its obnoxious owner are going to pay.

I've been listening to the bird for three days, ever since the mysterious neighbor in the apartment next door moved in. Under a writing deadline, I hadn't bothered to peek out the window at the new annoyance next door, doing my best to ignore the sound of boxes dropping to the ground and the constant milling about. I don't have to see the neighbor, though, to know whoever it is needs to leave. Between the shrieking bird and the blaring country music all hours of the day, I can't handle it.

Which is saying something, because I'm a girl who likes noise. I'm a girl of the club, of loud music, but even I am having an issue. A woman has her limits.

Stomping my feet as I get up from the couch, I yell to Sebastian, "I'll be back." The cat, who has gained at least five pounds since Avery moved out—probably in depression because his best friend, Henry the mastiff, left with her—doesn't move a muscle. So much for having my back.

Sliding my feet into orange flip-flops, I fling open my apartment door, feeling like a vampire as the sun shines down on me. I raise my hands in front of my face to shield my pale skin from the ball of light. I haven't been outside in days, feverishly writing.

I trudge across the narrow strip of grass between my apartment and the neighbor's, and beat my fist on the door, yelling "Hey," admittedly like a psychopath. I start to calm down a little, realizing what a fool I'm making of myself and how deranged I probably look, but it's too late.

The door flies open to reveal a man, probably about my age. He's got on a red plaid shirt, but it's completely unbuttoned. The first thing I notice after seeing his tanned chest and perfectly smooth jawline? His abs.

We're talking superdefined, six-pack abs. I hear myself inhale through gritted teeth, the sight of his perfect body only enhancing the tension within.

I shake my head, jolting myself out of the stupefied glance. I realize he's smiling, flashing perfect white teeth, eying my outfit. I cross my arms over my chest, feeling self-conscious now in my margarita glass shorts and cami set—sans a bra of any kind. Not to mention the leg hair I'm sporting like an accessory. Not my finest, most glamorous moment.

But it doesn't matter. This is war.

"Um, hi. I'm your neighbor and I'm here to complain about the noise you're making."

"Oh howdy, I wondered when you'd show up. Nice to meet ya. I'm Levi Creed."

His southern drawl is deep, the accent heavy enough to tell me he isn't from around here. Even if his voice didn't do it, the cowboy hat on his head would. And the cowboy boots. Who the hell wears a full cowboy getup in a beachside town… in summer?

He outstretches his hand to me. It looks like a strong, firm hand. I snub him.

"Listen, I'm not here to make friends. I'm here because your damn bird is ridiculously loud, as is the Johnny Cash music you've been blaring on repeat. I'm trying to work next door, and these walls are paper-thin, so…."

"Oh, sorry. Johnny Cash just likes his music loud." He shrugs, as if this is a normal admission.

I raise an eyebrow, wondering if this guy is high. His deep brown eyes aren't bloodshot, but who knows. He *is* wearing a long-sleeved plaid shirt, jeans, and boots in Ocean City in June. That's saying something.

"What?" I ask, shaking my head and squinting as if this will make his words make sense.

"Johnny Cash. My parrot. You want to meet him? He's actually pretty cool. A macaw. He can sing parts of a few of the songs, isn't that right, Johnny?"

The parrot lets out an infernal blare again before shouting "Hello" five times, and I'm brought back to my senses. This guy is out of control. It figures he would name his parrot Johnny Cash and then play Johnny Cash music for it. I can't even stand it right now.

"No, I do *not* want to meet your parrot. I want you to shut it the hell up because I'm under deadline. And, oh yeah, my new prospective roommate is coming later today, and I promised her the place is quiet and serene. I can't afford for her to say no because this place, if you haven't noticed, isn't the cheapest, and I'm not rich and can't afford to sit around listening to old-ass country music all day."

He stares for a moment in silence as I realize I've just unloaded perhaps way too much on this guy. I feel a little bad. Maybe I *am* just under too much stress.

His smile fades a bit. "Sorry. My bad, really. But listen, do you want to come in? The other neighbors came over with some kind of gelatin and weird casseroles, but maybe we can try them out. To be honest, I don't have any idea what they are. Never seen anything like 'em back home. What do you say?"

I blink at him, the guilt for my unloading gone. "No, I don't want to come into your honky-tonk bachelor pad and eat weird casseroles from the other neighbors who are apparently deaf because if I brought you a casserole right now, it'd probably be *poisoned*. Just saying." My hands rest on my hips, and even as I'm doing it, I know I'm being harsh. I know I'm just unloading on this guy, which isn't right. It isn't like me—although, I'm admittedly a bit rash and way too frank sometimes. And dammit, I hate country music. And obnoxious parrots.

Still, poisoned casseroles? *Too far, Jodie. Too far.*

But he doesn't look alarmed. He just shakes his head and laughs, which infuriates me even more. "Listen, we got off on the wrong boot. I'm sorry. Let's try this again," he says.

He turns, and I wonder if he's going to slam the door in my face. He doesn't. He walks away to the edge of the room. I notice as he does that he's limping quite awkwardly, making it seem like crossing the room takes immense effort as he drags his right foot and basically throws it with each step. A pang of guilt hits me, and I think about asking him if he hurt himself moving, but I don't. He makes it to the stereo, and the music stops, mercifully. He stumbles back toward me, the limp still prevalent. He smiles at me as he makes his way back to the door. I avert my eyes and make it seem like I wasn't staring at his leg. When I meet his gaze again, I realize he's standing way too close, leaning against the doorframe.

Then, as if we haven't just had this weird encounter, he simply says, "Hi, I'm Levi Creed. I moved here from Texas. Woodville, Texas, to be exact. My grandfather lives in Ocean City, and I'm here to spend some time with him this summer."

I sigh but find my glare easing up. Maybe it's the sight of him standing, still basically shirtless, in his tight jeans and cowboy boots. It takes some guts to pull off that look and still look—well, hot. The guy *is* new, and here I am ranting a mile a minute like a crazy person. He's probably thinking

I'm the one who's high.

I give in, take a breath, and reply, "I'm Jodie Ellison. I'm a writer, and a waitress at Midsummer Nights."

"A writer? That's awesome. What do you write?"

"Horror," I admit casually, averting my eyes.

"Oh, Jesus, so the poison thing might be something I should look out for?" He laughs, shaking his head and putting one hand atop his hat in an admittedly charming move. I'm guessing in my pixie cut and margarita glass pajamas, I don't exactly look like someone you'd have to worry about. Besides, he towers over me.

"I'm sorry. I'm just under a lot of stress. But your music *was* loud, and your parrot is obnoxious, just to be clear." I don't want him getting the idea I'm a pushover or a softie. Or that I was wrong.

"Understood. Listen, I hope things go well with the roommate situation. You won't hear a peep out of me all afternoon. I'll be the best damn welcoming committee you could ask for."

"Thank you. I'd appreciate it."

"Well, you better get back to work. Let me know if you change your mind about that casserole."

"Thank you," I say again, standing awkwardly for a second before backing away and taking the three steps to my front door. Once inside my apartment, I lean my back against the door, feeling like a maniac… and feeling like having Levi Creed right next door on the other side of these paper-thin walls might be trouble in more ways than just noise complaints.

***

I try to get some writing done once I'm back at my apartment. Sitting at my computer, though, I can't seem to stop worrying about Gemma Rayne and if this whole roommate thing is going to go as smoothly as last time.

It's not like I want a new roommate. I miss the hell out of Avery, but the solitude is good for the writing. It makes me focus—which is admittedly not my strength. Living with Avery was amazing, but it was also very easy to get distracted. These past months have forced me to focus on my writing when I'm home.

When the landlord jacked up the rent in March, though, it left me little choice. The book deal is signed, but I'm not quite rolling in the royalty checks just yet, since I'm only in the content editing stage. It's going to be a long time before—if—I see any sustaining money from this project— and that's if I can focus long enough to get these damn chapters redone.

The thought of a new roommate is daunting, mostly because I know no one is going to be as great as Avery. But Avery assured me this is going to all be good, and it better be. Because this Gemma Rayne girl was her idea, and if this crashes and burns, it's going to be all Avery's fault.

"I don't know. It seems like a bad idea," I said to Avery last month when she'd shown me an ad on Craigslist for an Ocean City roommate.

Avery leaned over the bar at Midsummer as I cleaned some glasses, the place closed for the night. Avery had cut down on her hours, and I missed the hell out of her during the day. Her new mural painting business was keeping her superbusy now—as was her supersexy tattoo shop owner boyfriend, Jesse. She made sure to stop in and see me though, enough that I didn't miss her too much.

"Are you kidding me right now? I mean, hello, the last time you used Craigslist, it didn't turn out so bad, did it?" she asked, grinning.

I shrugged and gave her a hand gesture that suggested otherwise. She scowled at me, and I laughed. "That's kind of my point, Avery," I said. "It turned out so well with you. What are the chances it'll work out again?"

"Hey, listen, it's going to be good. I mean, look at this. I emailed her, and she sent back more info. She just graduated college and is looking to come out to the coast because she's always wanted to live by the beach. She's in marketing for a well-established software company. She works from home, and she wants to relocate because she visited here on vacation a few times and loves the atmosphere. She doesn't have any pets and look, her picture is nice." Avery turned her computer so I could take a look at Gemma Rayne— which sounded like a stripper name to me. Not that I'm an expert on that.

Glancing at Gemma's picture though, she looked... innocent. I had to admit it. Her simple brown hair and smoky eye makeup complemented her huge, toothy grin. Her dark eyes sparkled, and she wore a hot-pink shirt. She looked clean, mature, and put together.

She looked like a far cry from the other roommate prospects I'd had so far. Still, I wasn't sold.

"She looks too serious," I said, dismissing the picture. "Look at her. She looks all prim and proper. I mean, who has a picture like that sitting around?"

"She's a marketing expert. I'm sure she had a headshot."

"My point exactly. Anyone who has a headshot just lying around that they email to people is too serious for me." I'd continued drying glasses, sighing, and shaking my head. "Plus, look at her. She just looks too perfect. She'll probably want to have weekly Bible study in my living room and sip tea all day. She'll be all judgy about my drinking and clubbing. I can't have some serious person living with me."

"Jodie, you're running out of time. You said yourself you need to get your finances together, and even though your book deal is awesome, you're not going to be seeing actual cash outside that small advance for a while. You need a roommate, and Gemma looks perfect. She's got a job, so you know she's reliable. She doesn't look like a serial killer. Give it a chance. It'll be great. Look how things turned out with me."

I thought about how last year, it was Avery who had found me on Craigslist. That had turned out well—I'd gotten a best friend out of it.

Could I possibly be that lucky again?

"She'll never be you, Avery. And if she is, she'll end up finding some supersexy tattoo hunk and moving out and moving on without me," I said, piling the guilt on.

Avery sighed. "I'm sorry. But in fairness, you did set me up with him. What did you think was going to happen?"

"Well, you two took it a little more seriously than I planned. I thought you'd get a fun night or two out of him. But no, I should have known Avery Johannas would be in it for the ring and the white picket fence," I teased.

"Hey now, we're not quite there yet. We're just living together."

I grinned and raised an eyebrow, taking her left hand in mine. I pretended to be shocked at the empty hand. "Another day empty! I better get a picture of this, because it can't possibly be this way for long."

"Well, I hope to hell he takes my advice and gets a princess cut, at least two carats. Otherwise, what's the point?" Lysander said, sneaking up behind me.

"You are all impossible," Avery complained, snatching her hand back. "And besides, we're not talking about me. We're talking about Jodie and her roommate situation. Lysander, look. What do you think of Gemma Rayne?"

"I think her name sounds like a stripper name," Lysander said.

"Thank you! Finally, someone is on my side," I said, putting a hand out to fist bump Lysander.

"What's wrong with a stripper? Maybe she could teach us all a few moves," Reed, Lysander's other half, said, sidling up behind me to get a look at the screen. "Oh, she's cute."

"Okay, why do I feel like we're on a bad dating game instead of real life?" I asked. "Let's play the let's-find-Jodie-a-decent-roommate-who-won't-kill-her-in-her-sleep game."

"Oh, you're paranoid. No wonder you're a good writer. Look at her. She screams girl next door. Give her a chance, Jodie. What's the worst that could happen?" Lysander questioned, slinging a bar towel over his shoulder before pouring himself and the rest of us a drink.

I sighed, leaning on the bar. I was running out of time, and soon the pathetic savings account I had would be in the negative. I had to give in, take a risk. Out of all my options, Gemma Rayne looked a bit serious, but probably the least likely to kill me in my sleep. "Okay. You're right. I'll email her and tell her to come as soon as she can."

"Well, good. Because I already told her she could come," Avery said, shrinking into herself.

"Are you kidding? Why would you do that?" I asked in disbelief.

"Because I figured you needed a shove. Come on, Jodie. It'll be great."

"So, when is Miss Stripper Name coming?" I asked. "And am I allowed to be there, or are you going to just pretend to be me?" I teased. I really wasn't mad. I knew Avery meant well.

"Next month. She has some loose ends to tie up in Chicago, but then she'll be here."

"Goodie. One more month of walking around in my underwear and leaving the milk sitting out on the counter, then I've got to get my shit together again."

"I'll drink to that," Reed said, throwing back his drink.

"You'll drink to anything," I replied before tossing down my own and hoping I wasn't making a horrific mistake.

***

"Hey, there! Oh. My. God. This place is adorbs!" the chipper voice practically squeals when I open the front door a few hours after the whole Levi Creed debacle. Thankfully, I've managed to change out of the pajamas and fix my smudged makeup.

Gemma Rayne stands in all her hot-pink glory. I have a flash from *Legally Blonde*, except much less adorable and without the cute little dog.

I try to be openminded, smiling and waving as Gemma dashes to hug me, a pink wheelie suitcase dragging behind her. "I'm Gemma Rayne. This place is cute. A little bit shabby chic, huh? I don't care though. I'm free. Away from the parents. Let's get this party started!"

She sings the final sentence and does some awkward little dance. I take a deep breath and paint on a smile.

I'm good at reading auras. I'm good at reading people. When Avery first came to my door last summer, I sensed an aura of kindness. I sensed a potential friend.

Right now, my aura reading for Gemma Rayne isn't screaming any of those things. It's screaming that this girl is trouble.

I calm my racing thoughts and tell myself not to be crazy. Of course she's not going to be Avery. It's not fair to compare her.

She brushes past me, dashing into my apartment—correction, apparently now our apartment. Looks like she doesn't have any issues with signing on as a roommate officially—as I'm left to close the door.

I inhale and again tell myself it's going to be great.

But twenty-two and wanting to get the party started doesn't sound good, and her over-the-top pink is already making me want to barf a little bit.

I know, Avery would tell me I'm a hypocrite. Party is usually my middle name. But reasonable partying. Late-twenties partying. Apparently, my Bible study, tea-party vision of Gemma was completely inaccurate. Perhaps the stripper name assessment was more in the ballpark than I could've imagined, judging by her scandalously short shorts and crop top. I might have met my match when it comes to being wild—and I'm not sure that's any better than a hymn-singing roommate. Not with "I'm away from the parental unit for the first time, let's get crazy" partying Gemma Rayne in the house. Why do I feel like this is going to start to feel like a sorority situation, me playing the role of campus security?

I smile, though, knowing I need this to work out and giving her the benefit of the doubt. It's all going to be good. Hell, she'll be so busy checking out the sights and sounds of the beach, I'll probably never see her.

"Oh no. Please tell me that's not a cat," she says, stopping, horrified. She covers her mouth and steps back from the couch, where Sebastian is sleeping on his back, his belly fat oozing over.

"Well, yeah, I told you in the email I have a cat," I say, confused. I'd sent a follow-up email after chatting with Avery just to make sure we had the details ironed out. I'd included a picture of Sebastian.

"Oh, I just sort of skimmed that. Because wow, I hate cats. H-A-T-E. Hate." She shakes her head in disgust, as if there's a dead fish on my couch.

She blinks at me, as if I'm just going to immediately kick Sebastian out. I blink back, arms crossed. "Well, I assure you, Sebastian is fine. Very sweet. I love him *very* much," I say, getting my point across.

This is it. I bet she's out of here, and then it'll be back to the drawing board.

Not like I'd be missing much. This girl already feels like a handful.

Still, she's innocent enough in her hot pink. I don't get any serial killer vibes, which is a plus. And she has a job, so I know she can handle her half of the rent.

I breathe, reminding myself roommates aren't easy to find—at least mostly normal ones. I can deal with a little girl drama, and I suppose I can forgive her for not loving Sebastian.

I suppose.

"Well, just so he doesn't pee on my stuff or really come near me, and I'll be fine, I guess," she says, as if she's the deciding factor.

"I assure you, he hasn't peed on anyone yet. Then again, everyone has liked him." I grin, but Gemma doesn't find my comment funny.

"Well, I'm not going to let a little *fleabag* ruin my fun. Show me to my room, and I'll get unpacking. Then I want to hit the sand. This is glorious," she says, smiling a huge smile again as if Sebastian has already been forgotten.

"Right this way," I say, feeling more like a bellboy than anything.

Gemma squeals at the sight of her room, which Avery graciously redecorated before she left, complete with a beachy mural. Gemma dashes in, tosses her suitcase down, and flops on the bed.

"It's good to be home," she says.

"Yes. You bet." I'm not sure what else to say as I feel my freedom and my rosy roommate image slowly dissipating.

Maybe I'm just afraid of change. There have been a lot of changes lately, I remind myself. I mean, really, how bad can Gemma Rayne really be? And with that new cowboy next door, I'm not sure she's going to be my biggest issue.

As if on cue, Johnny Cash lets out a squawk.

"Oh no, please tell me the neighbor doesn't have a parrot," Gemma says.

"He does. Is that a deal breaker?" I ask, wondering if I want her to say yes or no. I'm not sure.

She thinks for a moment and then shrugs. "It's not ideal. But I mean, I already have some of my stuff moved in, so I'll just live with it."

I blink at her. She's got one suitcase, a wheelie suitcase at that, in her room. That's it.

But if Gemma can live with it, I guess I can too. As she totes in box after box—one entire refrigerator box labeled "makeup"—I head to the kitchen to grab some coffee and decide to add a few extra shots of Baileys to it before helping her lug in the heavy boxes. Which turns into me lugging in the heavy boxes alone as Gemma eyes herself in the mirror, swearing she needs to fix her eyeliner and organize her makeup. She informs me she has a YouTube beauty channel and is a bit of an addict. She also asks if we have a bigger vanity than the one in the bathroom so she can properly organize.

As I inform Gemma Rayne that no, we don't have a vanity big enough for the entire Ulta store, I head to the kitchen. I think perhaps I had better restock my alcohol supply and take up meditation.

I'm in for a long ride.

Chapter Two

"That roommate you found me? She's got to go," I say through gritted teeth two days later when I'm working with Avery. We've both got a rare morning shift together—Lysander asked us if we could work since some of the college kids he just hired flaked out on him.

"Jodie, it's been two days. How bad can it possibly be?" Avery asks as we sit in the back on break, Lysander taking over for us for our fifteen. Midsummer is pretty slow since it's Tuesday. Lysander's been trying to push a Tuesday brunch menu, but none of us have the heart to tell him it's not really working. Right now, there are two tables filled and that's it.

"Let's see. She screams every time Sebastian goes near her because she swears he's trying to bite her. I actually saw her shove him away with an empty cereal box this morning like she was batting at a roach."

"Maybe she's just afraid of cats." She gives a half shrug.

"She refuses to call him his name and insists on calling him fleabag," I add, looking pointedly at Avery.

Avery frowns at this one. She's an animal lover and a Sebastian fan. "Okay, not ideal. But just ignore it. She'll get used to him."

"Oh, I could, if that were it. The girl drank all my alcohol and claims she thought it was community property." I feel my blood pressure rising at the mere thought of it. I mean, first mess with my cat… and then my alcohol? This girl is asking for trouble.

"Hey, I drank your coffee on my first morning."

"That was different," I argue. "You didn't touch my Jack Daniel's."

"Would we have been friends if I had?" Avery asks, grinning as she fiddles with an empty straw paper.

"Maybe not," I tease. "Anyway, I'm not done. She struts around our apartment in her underwear and bra all the time. I mean all the time—and I'm not even sure her underwear count as underwear, they're so tiny. I swear she makes sure Levi is in the front yard and can see her through the window when she does. Plus, she is demanding we redecorate the living room. Oh, and to top it off, I caught her on my computer this morning. My computer! My *work computer.* Unbelievable."

"Okay, hold up. Who's Levi?" Avery asks, raising an eyebrow and tossing the straw paper at me.

"Are you not listening to me? She was on my computer!" I can't believe Avery isn't hearing all this horrible stuff. Where's the loyalty?

"I heard you. Maybe she's just having trouble adjusting. Maybe you're just being tough on her because clearly no roommate could live up to me. She's got crazy-big shoes to fill."

I nudge her with my elbow, shaking my head.

"Now tell me who Levi is." She stares at me, demanding an answer.

"The other annoyance in my life. He moved in next door after Mr. Blossom moved out."

"Oh, I loved Mr. Blossom, but Levi sounds like maybe he's a little more eye-catching?" She winks at me.

"How do you know?"

"Because of the way his name rolls off your tongue. And the way you get so pissed about Gemma flaunting herself around him. He's hot, isn't he?" She nudges me with her elbow, which just annoys me even more. I exhale loudly.

"I don't know. He's okay. But that's beside the point. He is loud and annoying. And I swear he doesn't work. He's just over there, all hours of the day, and his goddamn parrot never shuts up. I confronted him a few days ago, and thank God, he's stopped blasting the Johnny Cash music. But he's still just aggravating. Listening to his television superloud or out on the front lawn singing to himself. The man is just… ugh."

"Uh-oh." Avery's face lights up.

"Uh-oh, what?" I ask. "Besides the fact that uh-oh, Jodie's life is falling apart and she's never going to meet her writing deadline with all this chaos."

"Not that kind of uh-oh. The uh-oh, Jodie's falling for a

man named Levi. When do I get to meet him?" Avery does a little shoulder shimmy that I find frustrating.

"You don't. It's not like that." I shake my head, exasperated that Avery's totally missing the whole point about Gemma and is hung up on Levi.

"But I think it could be," she says. "Come on, you complained about me last year being single. How long has it been since you've had some fun?"

"I've been busy. And I think I've been through the good stock in Ocean City," I argue.

"It's summer. That means freshly stocked fish," she says, winking.

I inhale, shaking my head, ready to give her a million reasons why she's crazy, ready to let loose and get rid of some of this pent-up anger.

"Oh, look at the time. Fifteen minutes is up. Better get back to work," she practically sings, dashing out the kitchen doors.

"It hasn't been fifteen," I say, shaking my head.

At least I got some of the Gemma situation off my chest. Something tells me, though, there's more to follow.

***

The sun beats down on me as I angrily sip my lemonade. I've got my laptop on my lap and sunglasses on, but the glare from the sun basically makes it impossible to see my screen. I've just got to hope I'm typing words at this point. I'll edit later.

Sebastian is in his cat harness, tethered to my chair. He

doesn't look very happy, but I figure it's better than leaving him in there with Gemma, all things considered.

I settle in, reminding myself a change of scenery can be good, listening to the sound of the crashing waves and trying to shut out the sound of honking horns and screaming children.

I've got to get these chapters finished.

When I came home from work, planning to spend the afternoon and evening writing, I found Gemma perched on the couch. She'd transformed the living room into what one could only call a set. There were lights perched atop curtain rods, and all my stuff was moved out of the living room, shoved in a corner. Her computer—one point in her favor, I suppose—was set up on a chair, a webcam aimed at her. She was wearing a suit jacket and her makeup was pristine.

Interestingly enough, she had yoga pants on the bottom.

"What are you doing?" I asked, closing the apartment door behind me.

"Oh hey, roomie. I have to get my YouTube video finished for the week. My followers are just dying for the eyeliner tutorial I'm doing."

"Can't you do that from your room?" I asked, confused.

"No. The lighting isn't good in there. Plus, it's sort of a mess. You know, all the boxes and stuff. Figured you wouldn't mind." She plastered on this huge, annoying smile I'm sure she's used to getting what she wants with. I felt myself glower.

"Well, I was going to write this afternoon," I responded through gritted teeth.

"Your room is free. It's not like I need that." She actually waved her hand at me as if she was brushing me off in my own house.

"I don't write well in my room. This is my spot," I argued, tension festering. In truth, I sometimes write at the coffee shop down the street, but I wasn't going to admit that to Gemma Rayne. I don't want her thinking she can just brush me off, kick me out of my own apartment whenever the fancy strikes her.

I honestly swore I'd give the girl another chance, ease up. But something about her grates on my nerves.

"You can't just write anywhere?" she asked, the valley girl voice emerging.

"No. Obviously."

"Well, I'll be done here in a few hours. It's a long tutorial, and I have to get a bunch of shots for before and after photos. Sorry." The last word rolled out of her mouth in a clearly sarcastic, unsympathetic fashion. I felt like she was channeling Regina George.

I sighed, muttering to myself about roommates and pink. Calming myself, I turned to her. "How many of these tutorials do you do?" I asked, wondering how long we were going to be playing YouTube star in my living room.

"Oh, about one a week at least." She primped her hair in the camera, making duck-faces at herself. Professional.

"Maybe we can work something out, then. You know, sort out the details since we both work from home so much." Now I painted on the sarcasm, hoped she'd get the point I was pissed and this wasn't going to keep happening.

"Yeah, we'll talk about it or something later," she said flippantly, as if perfecting her lipstick and smile in the camera were more important. "I've got followers to think about."

It's all good. You can handle this. You just need to get to know her. I'm sure she's not that bad, I told myself, breathing in and out. Gemma Rayne was a little—correction, very—trying, but she was young. She's just focused on her career. It's going to be fine.

But as I gathered up my computer after changing and grabbed Sebastian from my room—where Gemma had locked him, which was something we would be chatting about—I felt the anger rising. What was this? I was being evicted from my own apartment for hours while she did whatever she does? While she painted on eyeliner for her twelve followers? Infuriating.

But here I am. Being the bigger person, giving her space. Working under terrible conditions.

And getting nothing done.

Just as I'm hunkering down, though, and vowing to not let Gemma get in my way, a door opens. I turn around to see Levi Creed emerging from his apartment.

He's wearing jeans and boots again. And an open plaid shirt, his six-pack abs seemingly glinting in the sun. I swear he puts oil on them to make them even more noticeable.

Great.

"Howdy, neighbor. What's going on over here?" he asks in his deep drawl. I'd forgotten how deep his accent is.

I sigh, tossing my head back against the Adirondack.

"Oh, just trying to write."

"Out here? With your cat hooked to that contraption? I know writers all have their process, but this one is… interesting."

He walks over to a stone ring in his lawn, which I haven't noticed until now. He's still majorly favoring his leg. Must have been one hell of an injury. Probably from hauling all his country crap in. He leans down and starts stacking a pile of twigs meticulously in the center.

"What are you doing?" I ask, leaning up in my chair to get a better look.

"Cooking. Want to join me?"

"Wait, you're cooking out here?" I ask, putting down my laptop and craning my neck to see what he's doing. He's stooped down, his cowboy hat shielding his face from the sun.

"Yeah. Why not?" he asks, like I'm the crazy one.

"I feel like fire rings are like a safety violation. Pretty sure you can't start an open fire on the front lawn."

"Why not?" he asks, truly confused.

"Because you live in a city now. In an apartment building. You can't just go starting fires."

Levi shakes his head. "Sure have a lot of weird rules around here."

"Well, I'm just saying. You might want to check with the landlord. Wouldn't do to get evicted."

He gives a dismissive wave of the hand as if he's got more important things to worry about. Then again, it seems like not much is on his list of worries, judging by his attitude.

"It'll be fine. Easier to ask for forgiveness, you know?"

"Whatever you say. There are things called grills for a reason." I reach for my laptop to go back to typing. He doesn't talk for a while, but I still find myself distracted, my gaze wandering over to him too often. He's leaning down, starting a fire. As he stretches to get the paper in the fire just right, I notice how his jeans fit him in all the right places and....

"So, roommate thing not going very well, I'm taking it?" he asks, and I startle, hoping he didn't realize I was staring at him. I type a few words on my screen just to be convincing.

"Hardly."

"Never had a roommate, but I can imagine it isn't easy, especially if you get a girl like you have. That one looks like high-maintenance trouble."

Apparently her flaunting in front of the window has been working, because he's definitely noticed her. Then again, he doesn't seem to be impressed. Although, what guy wouldn't be? She's got the body of a twenty-two-year-old who only eats lettuce and works out fifteen hours a week.

I decide to cling to the first part of his statement, trying to block out Gemma's tendency to strut around half-naked. "You've never had a roommate? Ever? How old are you?"

"Twenty-seven. Good thing guys don't get offended by that question like women do."

"Sorry."

He stands up, wiping off his hands and admiring his flame, hands on his hips. He turns around to face me, hands still on his hips, abs still gloriously out. I force my eyes to meet his gaze, not his stomach.

"Don't apologize. Nothing to hide here."

"So you didn't go to college or anything?" I ask, willing myself not to openly stare in a lascivious fashion, trying to play it cool.

"Nope. Wasn't really my thing. Had other career plans. Lived at home with the folks until, well, this week."

"Interesting." I raise an eyebrow behind my glasses.

"Now hold up. Don't go getting all those creepy images of me living in my parents' basement, afraid to move on or mooching. In truth, I wasn't home much. My job kept me busy."

I put my hands up in the air. "Hey, I'm not judging. To each his own, that's all."

"You're judging. I can see it."

"Well, you judged me for sitting on my front lawn to write," I retort with some sass, even adding the signature Jodie head bob.

"Only because you have your poor cat strapped to your chair like a damn lawn ornament."

"Judging. See?"

He grins and shakes his head, putting a hand on his hat to make sure it's still there I guess. "You sure you don't want to join me for dinner?"

I think about it, eying the beach cowboy on the lawn beside me, thinking about how I could go for a marshmallow.

But then I think about the manuscript in front of me. "Maybe another time."

He shrugs. "Suit yourself." He turns to head toward his apartment.

"Can I ask you something?" I say on a whim before he goes, but when he turns around, I stop myself.

I'm sure his limp is just from moving, but it's probably rude to ask. What if it's the product of some tragedy? I put my foot in my mouth enough to know better than to go out on a limb.

Plus, more importantly, I don't want this flaunty cowboy to think I'm interested or something. I mean, what kind of man walks around Ocean City with an open plaid shirt? What kind of man puts a fire ring in his front yard to cook dinner?

I've been down the hot-bod-guy road before, and it didn't turn out great. He seems nice enough, it's true. But he's got that swagger about him, and I've seen that before. Something tells me Levi Creed isn't an innocent Texan boy. Something in his eyes, in his posture, in his everything screams rebel.

True, the last time I fell for a six-pack abs guy was at beach yoga, and the guy wasn't quite wearing a cowboy hat. But still. I know his type. A hell of a lot of fun… but a hell of a lot of trouble too.

The fire looks nice and inviting, but I've been burned before. I have my writing career to focus on. I don't need to end up in the burning embers again.

"Never mind," I say, and Levi stays put for a moment before smiling, tipping his hat at me like I'm some southern belle, then heading back into his apartment. He emerges ten minutes later with what looks to be some steaks. He sets up some kind of rack over the fire, and the smell is heavenly. I bury my nose in my computer, though, determined to get some work done.

When he's done cooking, he ambles back in his apartment, and I figure I won't see him again.

Fifteen minutes later, though, he comes out with a plate. "I don't want to distract you, but I had an extra and thought you might be hungry."

"Smells good. Thanks," I say, realizing I am actually quite hungry.

"One word of warning. More than one lady has fallen head over heels for me because of my amazing steak cooking skills. Eat at your own risk."

My mouth opens to spew some witty response, but I've got nothing. He winks at me, hands the plate to me, and once I take it, he spins on his boot and walks away, no further questions or comments.

I stare down at the plate, a fork and knife included. There's a heavenly smelling steak with a salad. Sebastian climbs up on my lap, pawing at the plate, almost choking himself on the harness in the process.

The man might have odd fashion choices, a southern drawl, and a bit of overconfidence, but ten minutes later when the steak's been devoured, I decide he can definitely cook a damn steak—and maybe Levi Creed as a neighbor has its benefits.

Chapter Three

"Are you off today?" Gemma asks me the next morning. I'm sipping coffee at the kitchen island, scrolling through social media. Sebastian is curled up by my feet. I notice her eye him as she talks to me, but apparently she decides he's not on the move, so she might be safe.

"Yeah."

"Oh, great. Me, too. Do you want to go shopping with me? I want to pick out some new décor. You know, more mature and stuff." She stands in her cut-off shorts and crop top, staring at me expectantly. She actually claps her hands.

I want to say hell no. I want to curl up on the sofa and binge-watch *The Bachelor* for hours or flip through magazines about fashion I can't afford and sex positions I don't have anyone to practice with.

But then I think about how I'm turning into some boring, stuffy version of Jodie. I'm too stressed and too serious. Where is my spontaneity? Where's my go-with-the-flow attitude? Just because my best friend moved out doesn't mean I should sulk around, and just because I'm struggling with my writing doesn't mean it's all Gemma's fault.

"Well, I could use some new shoes," I say, even though I have ten pairs sitting in boxes, not even worn yet. But hey, a girl can never have too many shoes, no matter what the organizing blog I follow tries to say.

"Oh, good. Show me where the best shopping is," she says, and I smile, heading to my room to change and hoping today could be a fresh start for Gemma and me.

***

Three hours later, my car is stuffed with bags of shoes, tank tops, toys for Sebastian, and a quote picture—I'm a sucker for quote décor.

Gemma's managed to fill the trunk with some weird elephant statues—her favorite animal, apparently—and some groovy rug she swears is chic. To each her own. I just made it very clear it was going in her bedroom. She pinkie swore it was, so clearly that must mean it's true.

Oh, to be twenty-two again.

We ate lunch at the sub shop Jesse introduced Avery to. Naturally, it also became my favorite. Hey, who can beat a $4.99 cheesesteak hoagie to die for?

Gemma passed, of course, ordering a salad instead. She's one of those girls, apparently. I try not to judge.

Overall, I must admit it's a good afternoon. I see the sweeter side of Gemma. Despite her cat-hating tendencies, her penchant for drama, and her wild girl trying to break free routine, I decide as we're unpacking the car she's okay.

Not Avery. Not best friend material. Hell, maybe not even lease-extension material.

But she's okay.

"Y'all need some help?" a deep voice asks from behind me as we're unloading the car. I turn around to see Levi.

Miracle among miracles, he's wearing a muscle shirt, no plaid shirt in sight. I must say I subconsciously am a bit disappointed that his glorious abs are tucked safely away.

"The beach boy in you emerging?" I ask, eying his free arms. And yes, the biceps are rippling, in case you had any doubt.

He smiles. "Figure I might ease into it, you know?"

He reaches for a few bags from my hand. Gemma looks over the car to appraise him. "Hey, I don't think we've formally met. I'm Gemma. Gemma Rayne."

Levi tips his hat at her—apparently, he's not ready to trade it for a sunhat just yet. "Nice to meet you," he says neutrally before loading his other arm with bags. I notice Gemma scowls a little at the lack of excitement on Levi's part.

He follows us into the apartment, dropping bags in the living room.

Sebastian opens an eye from his position on the couch. "Nice cat," Levi says, heading over to pet him. Sebastian rolls over dramatically, yawning, as Levi scratches his chin.

"Better than some squawky parrot," I mutter.

Levi rolls his eyes. "You don't even know Johnny Cash. I swear, he's a great guy."

"Not when he's screaming at six in the morning," I retort, meaning it. I apparently need to convince the landlord to invest in soundproofing. Or kick the parrot out.

Levi helps us carry the rest of the bags in. I notice Gemma swaying her hips just a little bit more dramatically when she leads us into the apartment.

When we're all done, I turn to Levi. "Thanks for your help, neighbor."

"Neighbor," he says, winking. "Does this mean you've accepted the fact I'm not going anywhere? Or maybe even like the fact? Knew the steak would work its charms."

"It means I'm thankful you helped me lug in our shopping haul. And don't worry, the steak didn't work on me like it apparently does some girls." I roll my eyes.

"Then it's just my Texan charm. I knew it'd win you over. Have a good afternoon," he says, smiling at me before letting himself out.

He's wearing another pair of excellent jeans, accentuated even more by the fact there isn't a plaid shirt taking away from the view this time.

"He's pretty hot," Gemma says once he's gone, snapping me out of the trance.

I shrug, trying not to admit I'm totally into his looks.

Because I'm not letting it go anywhere, I remind myself. Not that it would anyway. Levi said it himself. He's just being a gentleman.

"Too bad he has that awful limp. Is it permanent?" she asks. I whip around to eye her, wondering if I've heard her right.

"Wait, what?"

She rolls her eyes as she carries some bags back to her room. "Come on, tell me you haven't noticed the gimpy leg? Hopefully it's temporary because it'd be a real shame. To have that body but be defective? Gross."

She heads up the hallway as if she's just commented on a throw rug and not bashed another human being.

My jaw drops and I feel rage boiling up. "You don't even know him. What a bitchy thing to say," I yell down the hallway, not caring about niceties and keeping the peace.

I mean, Levi clearly isn't perfect with his loud music and open fires. But to claim he's defective because of his leg? I don't know his story. I don't know if it's temporary or permanent—and hell, I'll admit I'm curious about it. But not because I think it makes him any less attractive.

Gemma stops, turns, and looks at me. "Well, Miss Perfect, correct me if I'm wrong, but I don't think you really know him either. And it might be bitchy, but it's true. Are you telling me you don't think he's a little less hot because of it?"

"No, I don't. He's hot just the way he is," I bellow, fury bubbling. She rolls her eyes and stomps to her room, slamming the door.

So much for being okay, I think, before sinking to the couch. She's exactly the bitch I thought she was. I seethe, furious about the whole situation.

And then I hear a chuckle from Levi through the wall. The paper-thin walls.

"Shit," I mutter.

If I can hear his chuckle, he probably heard Gemma, which is terrible.

But then another thought hits me.

If I can hear his chuckle, he *definitely* heard me scream about how hot he is.

So much for not getting involved.

So much for keeping my distance.

So much for not letting Levi Creed get to me.

I bury my face in a throw pillow from the couch—a quote throw pillow—and scream as Sebastian jumps up on my lap.

***

It's the monthly Midsummer Night shutdown, so I've got the evening off. Once a month, Lysander insists on shutting the place down on a Friday night, even though that's our busiest night. He says it's worth the loss of profit to enjoy a night out with all of us.

Usually we all head down to the Marooned Pirate, our favorite club. Tonight, though, things are different. It's strictly a girls' night out because Lysander and Reed are celebrating their dating anniversary. They insisted it would probably be best if we went our separate ways tonight.

They didn't have to tell Avery and me twice. We've overheard plenty of kinky conversations to know we better leave those two on their own tonight.

It's been good to get out of the apartment and get some time with Avery. Things have undoubtedly changed since she moved out. No more late-night Netflix marathons or ice cream parties. It's been a little lonely, but I'm happy for her. I'm glad she and Jesse are doing sickeningly well since moving in together.

We've already been to a movie, a chick flick even Lysander and Reed thought looked cheesy—they're usually all about the rom-coms, but not this one. Now, we're at the Oceanfront Smoothie Bar, sipping on strawberry-mango drinks at the sandy bar, island music playing. Without Lysander and Reed's bad influence, we're semibehaving— Avery's idea, not mine. I wanted to check out the new strip club down the street, but now that Avery's officially committed, she's tightened the reins a little. Which is sort of a bummer, but I know Reed and Lysander will be happy to accompany me later this week. Regardless, I'm glad to be spending time with my best friend, whether we're ogling the male anatomy or simply sipping on smoothies—and besides, there are a few fine male specimens to ogle here at the Smoothie Bar, even though they have a lot more clothing on than I'd like.

"I miss Lysander and Reed and our margaritas, but this is nice. I've missed you," Avery says after slurping down some more of her smoothie.

"Miss you, too. More than ever." I stir my drink, and she cracks a smile.

"Still rough with Miss Gemma Rayne, huh?"

"You have *no* idea."

"Oh, I think I do. You've been complaining about her nonstop since she moved in."

"I'm sorry. I know I'm being a drag. It's just… she's

impossible. But no Gemma Rayne tonight. Let's talk about something else. How are things with green-eyes?"

Avery smiles, color spreading in her cheeks. "Amazing. Wonderful. I almost feel like I'm dreaming, it's so good. And I know that sounds cheesy and annoying, but it's true. I just didn't expect to find that again. Or find that for real, you know? I know it can't last forever and we're in the honeymoon stages, but still, I can't help but feel like Jesse and I could actually make it all work."

I smile. "I know you can. Why do you think I insisted on you getting that tattoo? You two were made for each other. You're good for each other. Even though it is a little sickeningly cheesy sometimes, we'll all deal to see you happy."

"We need to all get together soon. Jesse's been training the new tattoo artist, Phillip, with business at J & J's picking up and all. But one of these nights, we should go out."

"I'd like that. Although being the third wheel or, when Lysander and Reed come along, the fifth wheel, doesn't suit me." I take a sip of my smoothie.

"You know we don't see you like that. But if you're worried about it, get out there and date again. I hate that you-know-who made you gun-shy when it comes to dating."

"Speaking of Darren, he stopped by Midsummer yesterday," I say. "I forgot to tell you."

"Are you serious? What was he doing?"

I roll my eyes. "He was getting lunch with some new hot, perky blonde, one from yoga class. Apparently, he's making his rounds through the class. Unbelievable. Well, actually, quite believable now that I think about it." I shudder a little bit thinking about how stupid I was last summer, how even I let myself get swept up in some forever fantasy.

"Well, wonder if he got to George yet." Avery grins, and I start laughing, remembering the craziness from the yoga class. Never again will I force my body into weird positions just to impress a man—especially one who will end up cheating on me. "I hope you gave him the finger or something equally as sassy."

"I didn't have to. Lysander actually kicked him out. It was beautiful. Huge scene and everything."

"And you forgot to tell me?" She mocks horror. "I'm appalled."

"Well, Miss Painting Queen, come waitress with me more and you won't miss all the fun."

Avery sighs. "I love the painting business and that I've been getting more murals to paint than I could ever dream, but the downside is I do miss you guys so much."

"Well, you know where we all are anytime you miss us or want to see Lysander kick one of my ex's asses. So much for yoga making you strong. Darren ran away like a terrified ferret."

Avery raises an eyebrow. "A terrified ferret? That's your analogy?"

"Yeah, and let me tell you, his nether-region ferret isn't much of a prize. What was I thinking?" I shake my head, almost spitting up some smoothie at the horrifying thought.

Avery chokes on her smoothie, practically spitting it all over the bar. "Dear God, please do not tell me about

Darren's nether-region ferret. That's something I don't need to think about."

I give Avery my mischievous grin. "Yeah, I hear you. You've got enough action in Jesse's nether regions. Some of us, though, have to live in the past when it comes to their sex lives."

"Well, some of us happen to have what I've heard is a damn hot cowboy living right next door who would probably let you play a little rodeo with him."

"Okay, this conversation is over," I say, putting my hands up and feeling myself blush.

"Is Jodie Ellison blushing? What is this world coming to?"

"A world where cowboys live next door and my ex-roommate and current best friend keeps bringing him up."

"Well, if you'd invite me over to see him, I'd get off your case," she replies.

"Fine. Next time he's cooking on his damn fire pit, I'll call you over."

"Deal. If you also promise me one more thing," she says, that Avery Johannas fire in her eyes.

"What now?"

"You'll keep your mind open to the possibility that the wild man next door might be just what your own wild self needs."

"What's that supposed to mean?"

"I mean, Jodie, that you need a love that can keep up with you. By the sounds of it, the open fire pit, shirtless cowboy next door might be wild enough to run with you and keep you interested."

"I think there's some vodka in your smoothie. Now, are you ready? You promised I'd get to come see Henry for a little bit." I slurp the last bit of my smoothie out of the bottom of my cup very loudly and in a very unladylike manner. A few guys at the bar give me some interesting looks, but I don't care. Jodie Ellison is done trying to impress guys. She's learned her lesson.

"Fine. But let's get a pizza on the way. I'm starving."

And so, just like old times, we're off to our favorite pizza place for a late-night eating binge, like we're college kids or something.

But not like old times, after the pizza is gone and Henry's had enough ear rubs to fall asleep, I get up and go home, to my apartment, to a roommate who will never understand me like Avery.

And to the apartment that is neighboring that of Levi Creed, the man Avery seems to think is just who I need.

Chapter Four

"Are you sure you should've let Gemma handle this? From what you've told me, she just isn't the most trustworthy," Avery says. We're sitting at the kitchen island sipping coffees she brought. Avery's forehead is dripping with sweat, and she's trying to create airflow by pulling on the front of her shirt.

I'm wearing the skimpiest tank top and shortest shorts I could possibly find in my dresser this morning, but there's still sweat beading on my forehead, too, and dripping down all sorts of places I don't want to think about. I'm a hot mess, and I mean that quite literally.

It figures that on the hottest day of the year, our main air conditioner in the living room would break. Just figures.

Gemma's out at the local Home Depot getting a new one—after swiping my half of the money for it, of course. Apparently, when she was at the bar last week, some hot guy was there who works at the Home Depot in town. I wouldn't put her past breaking the unit on purpose for an excuse to go there.

Regardless, it's quiet without her, and Avery doesn't have to be at her new painting spot for a couple of hours. I've suggested we catch up on *Teen Mom* or *The Bachelor*. Avery has other ideas, insistent I lure the cowboy out of his apartment so she can get a look. I've shot the idea down. We've both considered having some real fun and letting Sebastian into Gemma's room. I can just imagine the horror in Gemma's perfectly lined eyes at the sight of the cat on his back right in the middle of her pillow.

"Hey," Avery says after taking another sip. "Speaking of Sebastian, where is my buddy? I haven't seen him, and come to think of it, he didn't greet me."

I freeze, looking at Avery before glancing around. I think back on the morning, realizing I haven't seen Sebastian, not since I got up and noticed it was hotter than hell in here. I remember feeding him his canned cat food bright and early, but after that....

We both leap to our feet and investigate, checking Sebastian's favorite napping spots. I find nothing but clumps of gray hair where Sebastian should be.

I start calling out his name, wondering where the big lug of a cat ended up. Avery dashes room to room.

And that's when I see it. The window. The wide-open window, the screen that was there this morning gone.

"Dammit," I yell, dashing toward the open window, hoping the fat cat didn't get very far. But I don't see him anywhere. Avery rushes to my side.

"Oh, shit," she says.

We wordlessly dash outside, frantically peeking around the apartment lawn.

And it's then I hear some wild parrot squawking above the country music blasting in Levi's apartment—so much for heeding my neighborly request to keep it down.

That's when I notice his window is, as usual, wide, wide open. He says real men believe in natural air conditioning.

"Is this the cowboy's home?" Avery says, her eyes glimmering despite the situation.

"You know damn well it is," I say. "But looks like he's not home."

I creep over to his window, peeping in to see Sebastian, all twenty pounds of him, climbing up Johnny Cash's cage, his claws fiddling with the door, the parrot screaming. Apparently he didn't get very far after his great escape. I can't even begin to imagine how he got his fat body through Levi's window and onto the parrot cage. Regardless, this is the predicament we're in now, and I have no idea how to get us out of it.

"Oh shit," I yell, waiting for Levi to come bolting to Johnny Cash's rescue. But he does nothing of the sort. He truly must not be home, despite the music blaring.

Thus, I do what any sensible woman would do. I try the doorknob, find it locked, and pound furiously on the door. We wait a moment, but detect no Levi movement. I kick the door in frustration.

Avery yells at Sebastian, hands on her face. "Jo, he's going to get the parrot. You need to get in there."

"And how do you suppose I do that?" I scream, in panic mode.

Avery looks at me and then peeks at the window. "Here, I'll give you a boost. You can just shimmy through there."

"I can't just climb through his window. Are you crazy?"

"You need to save the bird!" She is insistent, the take-charge Avery emerging in our time of crisis. I sigh and obey. She's right. Levi might drive me crazy, but I can't risk Sebastian hurting his bird—although if Johnny Cash bit the dust, it would be much quieter. Still, it wouldn't be the neighborly thing or the humanly thing to do.

Avery awkwardly makes a step for me out of her hands. "Apparently neither of us were cheerleaders," I say as we struggle and fumble on the front lawn. Finally, Avery practically tosses me to the ledge of the window, and I pull and strain to get myself through. The cat is hanging on the cage. At least he hasn't burst it open yet.

I finally slide through the window, and Avery claps behind me, apparently proud we've pulled off this James Bond—hardly—move.

I yell at Sebastian, flapping my hands at him, as I cross the living room floor. I'm almost at the cage when a door flies open inside, and footsteps come running toward me, probably to see what the commotion is.

The real Johnny Cash's "Folsom Prison Blues" is blaring as Sebastian meows at me, Johnny Cash the parrot screaming and flapping. Avery shrieks from the window, and says "Oh, my." I turn slightly to see Levi staring back at me wide-eyed.

But it's me who lets out the next scream, backing toward the window, because Levi is standing a few feet away from me, completely and utterly naked.

Like completely. Everything, everything, everything is hanging out for all to see.

And see it all we do.

It is only after a long, confusing moment he realizes what's happening and covers himself with cupped hands, but it's too late.

I've seen things I can't unsee, and maybe don't want to.

***

In the next few moments, a whirl of activity happens. I dash forward and grab Sebastian from the cage, hurriedly handing him through Levi's window to Avery so he can't escape again. She dashes back to my apartment, presumably to put him back and hopefully shut the window. Levi runs back for his bedroom, emerging with his signature plaid shirt and jeans. I stare, not sure what to do. Do I stay and explain myself or bolt? Levi comes closer and stands in front of me before I can choose. I consider the fact he's probably not wearing any underwear because he certainly didn't have time to put them on. Which means underneath those jeans—I cough, a sputtering cough made of nerves and tension.

I shake my head, jostling myself out of the lewd thoughts. "I'm… Sebastian… My air conditioning…." I begin, knowing I'm making no sense at all but having no clue what to say.

Levi turns off the music, and now there's just awkward quiet. He's grinning at me, hands in his pockets. I'm almost afraid to hear what he's going to say.

"You know, if you wanted to see me naked, you didn't have to come creeping in here with some excuse about your cat. You could've just asked," he says.

"I didn't know you were naked," I retort, feeling defensive. "And why the hell did you just come strolling out of there without clothes?"

He blinks at me before coolly replying, "Because it's my apartment and there wasn't anyone here. I was finishing up my shower when I heard some commotion and figured Johnny Cash might be in some sort of trouble, a wing stuck or something. I didn't think anyone would've broken into my apartment in broad daylight, so I thought I'd just take a peek and see what was wrong."

Well, this makes total sense. Not that I can admit that.

"Well, didn't you hear all the commotion before? I knocked before I came in." I am desperate to put the blame on him, to show him I'm not some pervert who broke into his apartment to eye him up. Although, at the moment, that is exactly how I must be coming off.

He shrugs. "I heard something but figured Johnny Cash was just singing."

"You really had no idea I was out here?"

"Whoa, hold up. I do believe you're the one who broke into my apartment. Sorry if you didn't like what you saw… or sorry if you liked it too much." The grin on his face widens. I reach out and smack his arm, scowling. He is unbelievable.

"Easy, cowboy," I say. "I was simply trying to save your parrot."

"What's your cat doing over here anyway?"

"He escaped out of our window. The air conditioning unit broke, and I put the screen in the window this morning, but I guess I did a crappy job because he got out and hopped in yours."

There's a knock at the door, interrupting us. Shit. What's Avery doing back?

Of course. She couldn't possibly let this opportunity go.

"I'll get it," I say, and Levi grins.

"Of course you will."

I answer the door. Sure enough, it's Avery, pink from the flurry of activity and probably from the sight.

"What are you doing?" I hiss.

"Figured I should rightfully introduce myself. You know, after all that." She giggles like a schoolgirl, clearly exhilarated by this turn of events. She gets to meet the cowboy after all. She gets to meet him in ways I couldn't have imagined.

"I reckon you've seen quite a lot of me already," Levi says, not seeming embarrassed as Avery bursts in.

"Oh my God, he *is* gorgeous. And that accent… and he uses the word reckon.…" She rambles on and on like some obsessed schoolgirl—and also like Levi's not standing two feet from us hearing every word.

"Avery," I hiss.

"Right, right. Sorry. I'm Avery Johannas, Jodie's old roommate and current best friend. Nice to meet you," she says, extending a hand.

Levi stumbles closer, his leg dragging behind. He shakes her hand, kisses it, and she swoons.

She's sold on him.

"Oh, he's great," she says.

Levi smiles and goes to tip the cowboy hat, which isn't on his head, a relic of his personal habit, I suppose. He smoothly puts his hand back down after he realizes his error. Without the hat, I get a view of his nice, full head of dark hair.

"Anyway," I say, trying to shift the conversation from Levi's hotness and Avery giving him the impression I rave about him all the time. "Seriously, Avery will tell you. I'm not lying about the whole cat story."

Avery smiles. Levi raises an eyebrow.

"Hmm," he says, crossing his arms.

"Are you serious? You don't believe me?" I reply, angry now.

He puts his hands out in front of him. He's still grinning. "I didn't say that. Just seems a little strange, you know. The cat climbed out your window and into mine? The same cat who does nothing but sleep every time I've ever seen him? Just interesting. But anyway, I'm glad you found him and everyone's safe."

I sigh, looking around the room. There is rope on the wall, and there's a huge saddle just sitting in the corner. I walk over to look at it.

"What's all this stuff for?" I ask. "You really take your cowboy décor to the extreme."

"That, my dear, is not décor. It's an actual saddle. I won many times on that saddle. It's kind of a legend."

Avery strolls over to look at the saddle, too, but now Levi's caught my interest.

"Hold up. You're a real cowboy?" I ask, looking at him as he leans on his good leg.

"Yup. At least I used to be."

"Like lassos and stuff?"

"Okay, not Wild West stuff like you're picturing. I was a saddle bronc rider."

"A what?" I ask, blinking like he's just told me he's from the moon. Avery shakes her head, telling me she has no idea.

"A saddle bronc rider. I'm guessing you have never heard of it?" he asks.

"Uh, not really?" I say. Avery hunches down to get a closer look at the saddle.

Levi sighs, shaking his head. He pulls out his phone and types a few things before motioning us over.

We watch a video of a cowboy on a horse as it bucks wildly. The rider clings on, bucking with the animal in a crazy dance. Levi pauses the video, and I stare at him in wonder.

"You do that?" Avery asks.

"I did." There's a seriousness in his voice, and his eyes drop. I'm in information overload right now, but suddenly it's all making sense.

"Is that what happened?" I ask, nodding toward his leg. I don't have to say it. He just nods.

"Yeah. Pretty stupid. I messed up big-time, took a real

hard fall. It's always a risk getting on, but you never think it's going to be you. I thought I was invincible."

"What happened?" I ask gently, not wanting to push too far.

"Broke my back. Doctors said I should've been paralyzed. It's a miracle I can walk again at all, really. The limp's not too bad when I consider all that. Still, my riding days were over right then and there."

Without thinking, I reach out and put a hand on his arm. I can see the pain in his eyes… I can see this was his dream. I can't imagine what it must be like to have it ripped from you. Avery steps back, pretending she's looking at the saddle again. She winks at me, and I shake my head. I pull back from Levi.

"It's all good. I mean, I miss it like crazy. It's the only thing I wanted to do. I trained my whole life for it. But sometimes life gives you no choice but to chase something new, which is why I'm here."

"I'm sorry. I didn't mean…," I say.

"To what? Let your cat almost eat my parrot? See me buck naked? Insinuate I'm a fake cowboy?" he answers for me.

I feel a tinge of guilt, but then he gives me a soft grin, the one I'm coming to know.

I smile back. "Right. Well, sorry for everything. I guess Avery and I best be going now."

"It was nice to meet you," Avery says, giving him a smile. "I'm sure I'll be seeing more of you."

"Not sure if that's possible," I say, grinning. Avery smacks my arm.

"In that case, I'm sure Jodie will be seeing more of you. At least I hope so," Avery says, smiling widely at getting in the last words.

Now I smack her arm. "Are you kidding?"

"Nope," she says, skipping out of the apartment, leaving me behind.

Levi shakes his head. "Anyway, thanks for saving Johnny Cash. I hope you can keep your cat over there. Apparently he digs my… what is it? Honky-tonk bachelor pad?" He uses air quotes, referring to the first day I met him.

I raise an eyebrow. "I think he likes my chic apartment better."

"Well, he did escape as soon as he got the chance. But I can't blame him with all that crazy estrogen happening over there."

"Whatever. I'll talk to you later," I say, shuffling toward the door.

"Nice seeing you," he says, in that charming accent that makes even those three words sound magical.

"Nice seeing you too," I say without thinking, and then I freeze. I squeeze my eyes shut and exhale as he laughs aloud. "I didn't mean it like that."

"Yeah, okay. Whatever you say." He laughs at my words, hands back in his pockets as he leans against the wall.

"Look, I've just never seen a real cowboy…." I pause there.

He's laughing louder.

"Not like that. I wasn't referring to the naked part and

all that. I was just…. You know what, forget it. I'm out."
But I'm laughing now, too, in spite of myself. I turn around
at the door to give Levi one last look, one last smile, and
then I close it behind me.

When I get to my apartment, Avery's standing in the
kitchen. She smiles the biggest smile at me. Gemma's flirting
with the Home Depot guy she's apparently convinced to
come and put the new unit in. They're over by the window.

Avery runs toward me, ignoring Gemma and the worker.
"Oh, he's perfect. Gorgeous. Funny. Sweet. He's great!"

"If you say so," I reply, but I can't help but grin.

"What are you two talking about?" Gemma asks,
strutting over in stiletto heels, her shorts short enough that
her butt cheeks are hanging out.

"Nothing. Just a little incident with Sebastian. I guess he
shoved the screen out this morning," I say.

"Oh, no he didn't. I popped it out to get better air flow
before I left. You were in the bathroom or something."

I take a step toward her. "And you didn't think Sebastian
was going to escape?"

She flips her perfectly curled hair—how the hell is it not
frizzy from this humidity?—shrugging. "Didn't think about
it. Not my fault your stupid cat isn't trained to stay in the
house. Who is this, anyway?"

She motions toward Avery.

"I'm Avery Johannas, your predecessor," Avery replies,
chin jutting out.

"Oh. So *you* painted the thing on my wall." She says it
like it's clearly not something she likes, her face scowling.

"If you're referring to the custom mural, then yes. The landlord, Mr. Earl, let me do it before I left. Said it would add value."

"Huh," she says, not gushing about the painting or saying anything. I actually think she shrivels her nose up.

"Well, anyway," Gemma says, flouncing back over to the Home Depot guy, leaning way too close as he tries to work. She never finishes the statement, acting like we're invisible. Avery and I walk to the kitchen.

"Okay, you're right. She's horrific," Avery says, turning her nose up. "I'm sorry. I was wrong."

"Told you. You owe me. Look at what I have to live with for the next eleven months, two weeks. Not that I'm counting."

"Well, I'll give it to you that I was wrong about that. But at least you have a next-door hottie as a bonus to get you through. Why don't you just move in with him, play roommates with that fine male specimen?" She winks at me creepily. I shake my head.

"You're impossible."

"Oh, come on. Don't be stubborn. You like him. I can see it in your body language."

"He's… he's okay. But a cowboy? Really? I don't know. He's not my type."

"Are you kidding? He's exactly your type, just dressed a little different. I mean, for God's sake, the man rode a bucking horse for a living. Can't get much wilder or more exciting than that."

"But that was the past. I don't even know what he does now. I don't even think he works at all. He's always over there."

"Details, details. With a bod like that, I don't care if he knits socks for a living," she says. "Now, speaking of work, this has been fun, but I've got to get to my next job. I'll be in touch."

"I'm sure you will. Thanks for your help, though."

Avery lets herself out, waving to me.

I shake my head, taking Sebastian back to my room, feeling hot and bothered, but probably not just from the lack of air.

Chapter Five

I'm plopping down for lunch on the sofa with Sebastian when there's pounding at the door. Gemma's out with the Home Depot guy, so I guess I'm relegated to the task of answering it.

When I fling it open, I'm greeted by Levi. He's wearing shorts, his legs pasty pale like they've never seen the light of day. He's still got on the cowboy boots and his plaid shirt. At least he's easing into this whole beachy wardrobe.

I raise an eyebrow at him, leaning on the doorframe, happy that at least I'm wearing a bra today.

"One, we really need to work on your beachwear. I applaud your effort at letting your legs see the sun, but come on. Boots with shorts? No. Just no. Isn't it hotter than hell in Texas? Didn't you ever wear shorts?" I ask before he can get a word out.

"Hey, I'm trying here. And no, it's not really advised to

wear shorts on a bucking horse. Plus, I'm a real man. Real men aren't bothered by the heat." He dramatically puffs his chest, and I roll my eyes.

"Anyway, can I help you? You're interrupting my soap operas." I pretend not to look at his rippling pecs.

He grins at me. "Actually, I'm here to help *you*."

I put a hand on my hip. "And what could I possibly need you to help me with?"

"Actually, it's kind of self-serving. I'm here to help you, which will in turn help me." He gestures toward the room, and I step back, letting him in, still confused as hell.

"Where's your washer?" he asks.

"Um, down the hall in the room on the right. Why?"

"Can't you hear it banging against the wall? It needs balancing."

"It needs what?"

He exhales. "I'm telling you what. Just show me where it is."

I lead him back down the hallway, feeling a little self-conscious about my messy room—bras strewn on the floor and such. I try to sneakily pull the door shut on my way so Levi doesn't get a full-on view of my undergarments as I usher him toward the washer.

"Here it is," I say, holding out a hand to the old, trusty washer I got on clearance when I moved in.

It's on the spin cycle, and now that he mentions it, it does seem to be hitting the wall a lot. I never thought about it. I guess I just assumed that was normal.

"That's what I thought. The wall it's banging against

happens to be my bedroom. As you can imagine, your early morning and late-night laundry gigs aren't great for the beauty rest. May I?"

"Oh, and your parrot and music blaring are good for my beauty rest? Give me a break," I retort, rolling my eyes.

"Well, at least we can fix this."

"I could fix Johnny Cash, too. I should've let Sebastian do the job."

"Then you'd have missed all the precious sights from yesterday," Levi says, smirking.

I shake my head. "Are you always this cocky?"

He chuckles at my word choice, which in hindsight might not have been the wisest.

"Oh my God, seriously? Are you fifteen?" I do smirk a little, though. It was poor word choice. Still, I try to act indifferent, like I'm super mature.

"Can I please just fix this damn thing?" he asks.

I put my hands up in the air. "Hey, if you want to be all handyman in here, be my guest. I'll be in the kitchen getting us some lemonade because I have no clue what you're doing. There's a bag of purple tools in the corner over there if you need them."

"And risk my masculinity using purple tools? I don't know."

"Oh, come on, cowboy. A bronc rider doesn't need to worry about his masculinity."

"An ex-bronc rider might, though. Just don't tell anyone, okay?" he says, reaching into the corner for my purple tool bag.

I smile. "Okay. Yell if you need anything."

About a half hour later, Levi emerges from the back room, wiping off his hands. I've been struggling in the kitchen, wondering if I should go back and offer to help—which wouldn't really be helping—or act all nonchalant. In reality, I snuck back to the bathroom to swipe on some makeup and fix my hair.

Which is absurd. It's just Levi fixing my washer so it doesn't drive him crazy. Avery's getting into my head.

"All fixed," Levi says.

"Thank you," I reply, eying his outfit again. I bite my lip, debating whether or not to say what I want to say. He did help me, though, so I definitely owe him.

Finally, I decide to just go for it. "I think it's time I help you out now."

"Oh yeah? How?" he asks, studying me.

"The only way I can. Get in my car. We're going shopping. You need some beach gear." In reality, I sort of just want to get out and get some new shoes. Still, it does feel like I owe him a little bit for helping. I would have no idea what balancing a washer even meant. A little shopping advice can't hurt, right? It's nothing too involved or intimate.

"I don't know. I'm not much of a shopper," he says, hesitating.

"You are now. Let's go. It's a public service to the entire Ocean City. You might be handsome and all, but no one can rock cowboy boots and shorts. No one."

***

"I don't know. I feel stupid in this. It's not me," Levi says, modeling a pair of cargo shorts and a tank top with a sun on it. He's also sporting some flip-flops and a sunhat.

I smile as I stand behind him, the sales guy at the local boutique nodding.

"It looks good. Trust me," I say, trying not to let on just how good I truly think he looks.

"All right. Who am I to argue with a true beach girl? I guess I'll take it."

"Yes. See, look at me, helping you assimilate into beach culture."

"Just don't think I'm getting rid of the hat and boots. This will just be a look I'll try out," he says before heading back to the fitting room.

After we check out—I of course find myself a new pair of sandals—I lead Levi to a tiny café down the street famous for its omelets.

I convince Levi to order a Western omelet even though it's two in the afternoon. As we're waiting for our food, me sitting across from him in a booth, I start to fiddle with a straw paper, realizing this whole scene could feel intimate, date-like.

It could. But it's not. This is just two neighbors out for some fun. This is *just fun*. Stop analyzing, I remind myself.

"How is the writing coming along?" Levi asks me.

I look up at him, deciding to be honest. Something in those brown eyes makes me want to tell him the truth. "Not great at all. I'm under deadline for a content rewrite and, well, it's sucking. I can't find my groove. I feel like I've lost my touch or something."

"I'm sorry to hear that, but I'm sure it'll come."

"I hope so. I'm set for release early next year, but at this rate, I don't know."

"That's awesome. I've never known an author before." He smiles at me, looking genuinely happy.

I shrug. "It's not for everyone, I guess. It takes a long time to build a career in it. Lucky for me, though, my mom encouraged me from the beginning. She told me to go after my passion, so I did. I might not be rich or super successful at it, but I love it. It's worth it, no matter what."

"Sounds like your mom is a great lady."

"Yeah," I say as the waitress brings us our coffees. I stir in some creamer as I talk. "She really is. She's not the super clingy kind of mom, but she's always been there for me when I need her. She's super fun and super spontaneous."

"What about your dad?" Levi asks, not putting any creamer in his coffee.

"Don't know him. He took off when I was born. It's just always been Mom and me. We lived about two hours from here. Mom's a bit of a wanderer and an artsy kind of person, so that's where I get my creative side, I think. She's actually in Europe right now. She quit her job a few years back to be a travel blogger. She's also got the writing bug."

"That's awesome. Sounds like you're grounded in your roots," Levi says, blowing on his coffee before taking a sip.

"How about you? Tell me about your family," I say, because it feels like the natural way to take our conversation. Plus, I'm curious. I realize I don't know all that much about the Texan sitting across from me who lives beside me. I really don't know that much at all, which seems like a shame.

Levi shrugs. "Mom and Dad own a small law firm back home. I grew up in Woodville, which is a town that has that Texan charm. There were quite a few rodeo cowboys living nearby, so I think that's part of the reason I got interested. Mom and Dad weren't really into the whole ranch thing or rodeo thing, which probably only lit my interest in it even more, to tell you the truth. Had a friend in high school named Bill whose family had a ranch. I'd sneak over there all the time, and his dad would teach me the basics of rodeo. I was hooked from the first time I went there. The parents weren't thrilled when they found out, but they couldn't stop me. By then, it was a done deal. I was hooked on the adrenaline and the danger. They wanted me to follow in their footsteps, be more practical, go to law school."

"But were they supportive of your rodeo days once it got serious?"

"Not really. They never thought it was a real career. Mom always thought it was too dangerous. I've always been a bit of a rebel, though," he says, smirking now. "Liked to live on the edge, to do things no one else would. And I was always good at it. When I got hurt, I think they were a little relieved because it meant I'd have to move on with my life and find something else."

"Which is?" I ask.

He shrugs. "I'm still sorting that out. Right now, I guess you could say I'm looking at going the business route."

"And your grandpa lives here, right?" I ask, interested in his story.

"Yeah. Mom's dad is the one who lives here in Ocean City. It was my grandma's dream to live here, but they never did. When she died about six years ago, he moved here and never looked back. I decided after the accident I might as well follow in his footsteps, see what the beach was all about. Seemed like a good change of pace, like a new adventure."

Our omelets come, and we start scarfing them down. I didn't realize how hungry I was.

"Do you have a girlfriend back home?" I find myself asking. I internally scold myself. This is what you ask someone when you're interested. I don't want him to misinterpret this. "Sorry, you don't have to answer."

"I did, before the accident. Let's just say when things fell apart for me, things fell apart for us. But it's all good. Looking back, I was too serious, you know? I've learned from this whole thing it's better to be flexible, not box yourself in. After things fell apart, I vowed to myself to just have fun in love and not be worried about commitments. You know, the whole no-strings-attached thing?"

I think I literally exhale the breath I've been holding. No strings attached. Pure fun.

Sounds right up my alley.

"Oh, I know. I'm in the same boat. Last year, I thought maybe I was starting to feel differently, but then I got burned. Love sucks, you know?"

He nods. "I think dating and relationships are overrated,

you know?"

"Spoken like a true rebel," I say, and he lifts his coffee in a mock toast.

"To the rebels, and the wild hearts in their chests that refuse to be tamed," he says.

I grin. "To the wild hearts, may we forever be free and roaming."

We clink mugs, and a wave of relief washes over me. This whole thing—whatever it is with Levi—is fun and exciting, and now I don't have to panic. Because no matter what, I know we both feel the same way.

No to relationships. No to commitment. Yes to a whole hell of a lot of fun.

Because what else are your twenties for? We finish our omelets and head home, a new ease forming between us now that we know without a doubt this whole neighbor thing isn't on the cusp of becoming something else. Still, as we amble toward the car, Avery's words about wild hearts comes to mind.

Clearly, though, Avery doesn't know as much as she thinks, because Levi and I are just living it up, having fun, and not worrying about tomorrow or the future or forever.

***

We head home, returning to Levi's apartment with handfuls of bags.

He's now got shorts, swimming trunks, muscle shirts, T-shirts, and sandals. Everything an Ocean City man needs to blend in.

"Well? What do you think?" I ask as I help him carry in some bags.

"I think you enjoyed dressing me up like a Ken doll too much," he says. "But I'll give it a try."

"Come on. You know those jeans and boots are too damn hot. Besides, how the hell do you manage on the sand in them?"

He shrugs. "Haven't really been on the sand yet."

"Are you freaking kidding me?" I ask, truly stunned. Okay, in fairness, I'm no beach lounging rat, either, but I make my way to the water at least a few times a week. "Well, we're changing that. This week. I'm taking you seashell hunting."

He grins. "Okay. But one question."

"What's that?"

"Can I still wear the hat with the whole beach getup?"

I smile. "I wouldn't expect anything less. Of course you can. Now I should run. Work beckons. Thanks for all your help."

"Same to you."

I smile and leave, heading to get dressed for work. Maybe having Levi next door is a good thing after all.

Chapter Six

"It's weird being out without Lysander," I say as Reed hands me a margarita.

"And without Avery. Guess it's just you and me, kid," Reed says, clinking our glasses as the music at the Marooned Pirate blares.

It's a Friday, and I've managed to snag the night off, having worked this morning. Lysander is working, and so is Avery. Reed and I thought about kicking back at a table at Midsummer, but Lysander wouldn't hear of it.

"Get the hell out of here, go have fun for all of us," Lysander ordered from behind the bar.

Reed had shrugged. "Well, you don't have to tell me twice to go party. Come on, Jodie. Let's go."

So here we are, walking into the club like a couple even though one of us is very taken—and not into women at all. Sitting on the barstool, though, it *is* good to be out of the house. I've been buried in writing and work the past few weeks. It's good to shake it off and have a little fun.

Reed and I make our way to the dance floor, dance to a few songs, and toss back quite a few more drinks. A couple of guys wander over to talk to me, but Reed gives me the signal—a readjustment of his collar—to tell me they're creeps or not worth my time. I trust his judgment, probably too much.

"Why didn't you bring the sexy cowboy?" Reed asks later when there's a lull in the music and we're perched back on the bar.

"Let me guess. Avery's been raving about him."

"She did say he's got quite the bod. Lysander and I are dying to meet him. Avery says he's a real hunk and quite perfect for you."

"Okay, I'll admit he's hot," I say, the alcohol loosening my lips and dulling my brain. "But I'm not looking for a relationship. And it's probably not the best idea to have a one-night stand with a guy I have to live by, you know?"

"No. I don't know. I think you're crazy. He's hot. You're single. What's the problem?"

"Come on. I know guys like him. All the sexy ones turn out to be assholes. And I don't want to have to live by him when things fall apart."

"Miss Doom and Gloom. You have no idea it'll fall apart. Come on. Stop being melodramatic and have some fun already. What's the worst that could happen?" Reed orders us another round of drinks.

"It's getting late. Shouldn't we be going?" I ask as we

wander to the bar to take a break from dancing a little later.

"Wow, you *are* getting boring. No way. Lysander texted. He and Avery are cleaning up and then they're on their way for a round. So you better get your ass ready for some more partying, because I think it's going to be a late night."

I sigh, then smile. "You know what, you're right. This is what the twenties are for, right?"

"And the thirties and forties," Reed says, smiling.

A half hour later, Avery and Lysander stumble in, and I run to meet them, wrapping my arms around them both simultaneously. "It's about time you two got here. Let's get this party going," I yell.

"Someone's had a few drinks. Reed, how much alcohol did you force her to consume?" Lysander asks as we all approach the barstool Reed's on. Reed gets up, and he and Lysander start making out shamelessly.

"Okay, you two, cool it. You've been apart for what, a few hours? Jesus. Keep it together until you get home," I say, shaking my head but smiling.

They finally pull apart, Reed kissing Lysander's cheek. "Oh, come on. In a few months, it'll be you needing a room with Levi."

I open my mouth in mock horror. "Will you all stop? You're all becoming obsessed with him, and you don't even know him."

"I've always thought it would be hot to date a true cowboy," Reed says. Lysander playfully nudges him. Reed puts his hands up. "Before you, of course."

"Gag. You two are too much in love. Speaking of

lovebirds, where's your other half, Avery?" I ask, trying to change the subject.

"He's on his way," she says as she sidles up to the bar to get the bartender's attention.

"Well, this is going to be quite the night. Let's get things going, what are you waiting for? Get a drink in your hand and let's hit the dance floor!" I scream, enlivened by the night. I order a margarita for Avery and another Long Island for myself.

When Jesse arrives and is hanging on Avery, I yell out, "Fifth wheel, coming right up!" and run to the dance floor, shaking it like I'm Shakira—even though I can't dance when I'm sober, let alone when I've had as much alcohol as I have.

But screw it. I've been responsible and hardworking these past few weeks. I've dealt with an awful roommate and all sorts of tension with the guy next door and everything else. I deserve a night to be free.

So I live it up. We stay at the club until about three in the morning, all having enough drinks to cause our livers to float away. I dance with a few hot guys, but to Lysander and Reed's utter disappointment, it doesn't go anywhere—as in, no one gets invited to come home with me. When we've finally reached the point of exhaustion and I've managed to dance on the bar like I usually do when I'm emboldened by too many Long Islands, we call cabs and head out. The two couples head home to probably have some hot alone time, and I return to the apartment to snuggle up to my cat.

A little sad, I know. But it's all good, I convince myself.

As the cab drops me off, I look at my apartment and then look at the door next to it, wondering what Levi's up to.

Wondering what it would be like if I turned to the door to my right instead of the door to my left. I feel like the girl in the "Lady or the Tiger?" story, but I know the ending.

I go to the left, my drunk ass understanding this is the wise choice, the responsible choice, and the safe choice.

But when I open the door, my eyes almost bug out of my head.

"What the hell?" I scream, because even in my inebriated state, I know shit has gone very, very wrong here tonight.

There are probably a hundred beer cans crumpled in the apartment. Hoodies, broken wine cooler bottles, and cigarette butts are everywhere. Like truly everywhere.

I wander over to the couch; my magazines and books are strewn about. There is a lacy red thong on the couch that doesn't belong to me. I stomp down the hallway and find the door to my room shut. I take a breath and fling it open. Mercifully, my room is in good condition, Sebastian meowing at my feet in desperate loneliness after apparently being locked in all evening.

At least she had the good sense to keep everyone out of my room. But what in the hell happened here tonight?

I storm back to her room, not caring if I'm invading her privacy, not stopping to think she could be with someone in a compromising position.

I fling her bedroom door open.

There are two bodies in the bed. I don't care, partially emboldened by the alcohol, and partially emboldened by the anger boiling in my blood.

I flip the light on, and Gemma lets out an infernal groan that sounds like death itself.

In bed beside her, the Home Depot guy sits up. I shield my eyes, not wanting to see anything I can't unsee.

"Gemma, what the hell happened in here tonight?" I demand from the doorway, shouting into the room.

She moans. "What time is it?"

"Answer the question," I demand, putting a hand on my hip.

"We had a little party," she mumbles.

"You trashed the house. It's a disaster." I lean on the doorframe now, feeling a bit woozy but needing to have my say.

"It's fine. I'll get it tomorrow." She flops over onto her side.

"You're damn straight you will. What were you thinking? You're lucky no one called the cops."

"Loosen up. We were having fun. It's my apartment too." She slowly sits up now, and the Home Depot guy rolls over in bed beside her.

I seethe, anger roiling inside at an unhealthy rate. This is going nowhere productive, and I'm too tired to deal with it all right now. "I'm going to bed now. Tomorrow, your ass better be cleaning this place. *Unbelievable*. You know, they do make these things called clubs. If you want to party, you should try it sometime."

I pull her door shut with a loud thud as I channel my annoyance into the action. Head pounding, I stomp to my room, locking Sebastian in with me. I don't want him getting into the disastrous mess out there.

But as I climb into bed, I let the anger dissipate. I'm exhausted, and tomorrow's not going to be a good day. If I'm lucky, I'll spend the day making sure Gemma puts the place back in order. If I'm not lucky, someone called the landlord and I'll be getting an eviction notice.

Either way, the sun will be coming up soon, so I'm going to go to sleep and do what I do best—worry about it tomorrow.

***

When I finally peel myself out of bed the next morning, it's around noon. I stumble to the kitchen, looking for my breakfast—coffee and Advil.

Gemma's already sitting at the island looking like nothing happened last night. Apparently Home Depot guy has wandered out. She's showered, and her hair is wet and hanging down her back. She looks perky and perfect.

Damn those early twentysomethings.

I want to scream and yell at Gemma, who also has coffee and Advil for breakfast. Although, I can't help but notice she only needed one dose of each, and she's looking pretty chipper. I suppose a twenty-two-year-old's hangover is a bit easier than a twenty-seven-year-old's. It figures.

It makes me hate her even more.

We wordlessly stare at each other for a long moment, the sun seeming way too bright. I glance around, hoping my drunken stupor made everything seem worse than it is.

It didn't. It's just as bad if not worse than I remember from last night.

Besides all the garbage I noticed last night, there's also major damage.

My gaze lands on a hole in the living room wall where apparently someone got crazy. The handle on the fridge is snapped off, tossed on the counter beside a pile of empty red cups. There are blotchy stains on the carpet. Pictures are crooked or on the ground, scattered about haphazardly. I think there's a cigarette burn on the island. It looks like a natural disaster, or like it should be condemned. My apartment, in short, is barely recognizable. I was never a neat freak, to be fair—but this is well beyond a "lived in" look.

I bury my head in my hands for a moment, closing my eyes and hoping everything will vanish when they open.

This, of course, does not happen. This is no magical wizarding world or magical anything.

"Look, I'm sorry," Gemma says sassily when I glare at her wordlessly. "I didn't mean for it to get out of hand. It's just... I wanted to have fun, you know?"

"I know. But like I said, that's what clubs are for. If the landlord sees this, we're going to be in trouble."

"I'll fix it." She shrugs and sips her coffee, as if I've suggested she do a load of laundry or some other mundane task. She acts like this is a five-minute job, which it clearly is not.

"Oh really? You know how to fix drywall?" I raise an eyebrow.

"I'll pay someone to fix it." She shakes her head as if I'm the biggest idiot in the world.

"Oh, you're rolling in cash now?"

"Not after last night. Beer is expensive, you know. But come on. I'm sure I can get a discount at Home Depot after last night." She winks at me, and I try to keep myself from dry-heaving.

I roll my eyes but then think about myself last night. The expensive margaritas I threw back like they were free. The crazy dancing and the wild times. I can't judge Gemma too much.

Not *too* much.

Although I didn't cause damage to the apartment in the process.

"Look, let's get to work. I'll help you," I say through gritted teeth, the hangover apparently dulling my sass and intelligence.

"You're going to help me?" Even Gemma is shocked by the prospect.

I sigh. "You're not the only one to be stupid in her early twenties. If I'm being honest, I've had my share of stupid, out-of-control parties. Just don't do it again."

"Of course not," she says, but the way she averts her eyes tells me she'll be doing it again.

And then, the claws will come out.

That's another argument for another day. Right now, my goal is to get this place cleaned up so that if the landlord gets a complaint, it'll be back in good shape before he can even see it.

We start bagging up trash, Gemma in the kitchen and me in the living room.

I take the first bag outside to put in the dumpster out back. As I squint at the sun, I hear, "Howdy. Some party you two had last night."

I turn to see Levi, in his shorts, sandals, and T-shirt. "Nice outfit," I say, my voice grating.

"Thanks." He's sporting bags under his eyes and looks exhausted.

"You look tired," I say because my head's still throbbing and I can't come up with anything better.

"Yeah, like I said, it was some party next door. Hard to sleep with all the yelling, you know?"

I rub my head. "Sorry. I wasn't home. Gemma… she apparently got a little out of hand."

Levi eyes the bag in my hand. "I'll say."

"I'm sorry. Won't happen again. We're just cleaning up. Please don't report us."

"For partying all hours of the night? Playing music too loud? Now what kind of neighbor would I be to complain about that?" He shoots me that infuriating grin. Mixed with the pounding headache I still have, it's too much.

"I get it. I'm sorry. But please, I don't want to get evicted."

"No worries. I was just a little sad I didn't get an invite. Sounded like a blast over there. But I have to say, if you weren't home, where were you? Because you don't look all chipper this morning either."

"Out. The club," I admit.

"Sounds… interesting," he says.

"What? You're not a club kind of guy?"

"Oh, I am. But probably not your kind of club. I feel like maybe we do it a little differently back in Texas."

"And how do you know what kind of club is my kind of club?" I ask, still holding the trash bag.

"Let me guess. Pumping music, scandalously clad women, girly drinks, and a whole lot of grinding and twerking you like to call dancing to some beats and talking you call singing."

I open my mouth to argue, but after a second, I realize he's basically described my club experience. "Okay, yeah, but what's wrong with all that?"

"I mean, nothing. Especially not the whole scandalously clad part. But, it's just not my scene. We do things a little differently back home."

"By differently you mean all country western, *Footloose* style line-dancing? Yeah, sounds *so* much better." I roll my eyes.

"Now who is being judgy?" He smirks, throwing my own accusations in my face.

I shake my head. "Well, I have about a hundred beer cans to pick up, so if you'll excuse me."

"You want some help?" he asks. I think about taking him up on it, but then the independent woman kicks in.

"I've got it. Besides, I don't want you having ammunition to show the landlord."

I head to the dumpster, heave the bag in, and trudge back inside, staring at the impossible task before us. It's going to be a long, long morning followed by a long, long afternoon of waitressing.

Chapter Seven

Later that evening, I'm coming home from a shift at Midsummer when I see it.

"Shit," I mutter under my breath as I hang back around the corner of the apartment complex.

I have only seen him a handful of times, but it's enough to know I'm not crazy.

It's the landlord, Mr. Earl. And he's heading into Levi's apartment.

Once he's inside, I dash inside my apartment. This is it. Levi's turned us in. He's called and reported Gemma and the party. So much for all that small talk this morning, making like he was cool with the party. What a liar. What a no-good, two-faced liar. How could I have been so stupid to trust him?

Any minute, Mr. Earl's going to be over here demanding answers and dishing out consequences.

I rush back to Gemma's room, but it's empty. Figures. The work-at-home girl is nowhere to be found on a day I need her.

I glance around the place, wondering if I can pull off the

"what party?" lie. At least all the trash is gone. I eye the wall where the hole was… I shoddily slapped up a poster of Adam Levine that Gemma had in her things. It's clearly out of place hanging sort of near the baseboard in a super-odd spot on the wall, and it's probably pretty clear it's covering damage.

There are still some wine stains on the carpet that won't come out. I move the throw rug over, again to a very conspicuous place, but it'll have to do.

Then there's the refrigerator handle. It's duct-taped.

I sigh, plopping on the couch, sitting very still. I try to eavesdrop on the conversation so at least I can be prepared, but the damn parrot is squawking again. I hear a few words about "repairs" and "learn your lesson." That sounds foreboding. I also manage to hear Levi laugh a few times, which infuriates me. So much for this whole connection thing I thought we had going. So much for trust.

Wait until I tell Avery she was wrong yet again.

The minutes tick by, and nothing happens. I sit in a nervous sweat, not even bothering to move, staring at the door.

And finally, a half hour later, I hear Levi's door slam shut. My stomach plunges in anticipation.

The knock comes. I take a deep breath. Here it goes. I hope Jesse and Avery have a couch I can sleep on, and I hope Gemma and the Home Depot man are as close as she claims.

I march to the door like I'm marching to my own funeral, fling it open, and wait for the gavel to fall.

Instead, I see Levi standing at my door.

Fury rises. "So, you rat me out to the landlord and then you march over here to brag? Real classy," I say, slamming the door in his face

He puts out a hand to stop it, though, and damn he's strong.

"Easy, Jodie. What are you talking about?"

I glare at him, stomping to the middle of my living room. "Don't play games. I saw Mr. Earl over at your apartment. I'm not stupid. The party last night? What, is he drawing up the documents to have us evicted?" I gesticulate wildly with my hands, anger driving my every move.

Levi shakes his head and chuckles.

I just continue. "Glad you think it's funny. Some of us can't afford to be kicked out. Some of us can't lie around napping and cooking on fire pits all day. We have jobs, and we have bills to pay. Some of us have a finite amount of cash and need to keep our living arrangements."

"Easy. Jeez! You've got it all wrong."

I put a hand on my hip, jutting it out, hoping I look formidable—in reality, I probably look silly and dramatic. "And what do I have wrong?"

"Everything. For one, I don't lie around cooking on the fire pit. I do work, you know."

"Really? Because it's not like I see you regularly leaving for your nine to five."

"Did you ever think I work from over there? Or that I have a job that isn't nine to five? And how closely are you watching me? Should I be worried?" He smiles that infuriating grin.

I bite my lip, scowling. No, I hadn't thought of any of that, actually. "Don't change the subject. This is about you ratting me out. Look, I'm sorry about the whole party fiasco. But turning me in? Really?"

"I didn't turn you in." He stands, hands in his pockets in the middle of the living room, that smile that's usually hot just enraging now.

"Then what were you chatting with Mr. Earl about? The flower garden out front? The rising rent prices?" The sarcasm drips from my words.

"Actually, yes and yes."

I sigh. "Come on."

Levi smiles. "Grandpa likes to keep me in the loop about all the decisions he's making, since I need to learn the ropes."

I freeze, tilting my head. "Wait, what? Did you say grandpa?"

"Yeah, I did. My grandpa's the landlord. My mom's dad." His hands still in his pockets, he says the words like it's the most obvious statement he could make. He acts like this is widely known news, like it's not a big deal at all.

I stare for a moment, waiting to see if there's a punchline or if he's trying to be funny, but he just shrugs. I shake my head, averting my eyes to the ceiling and exhaling loudly. This is just great.

"Oh, isn't that *dandy*," I finally say when I've wrapped my head around the concept. I emphasize the last word. "You're here, pretending to be all Texan and clueless about the beach, when really, you're here to spy on us for your grandfather and make sure we're staying in line. Unbelievable."

Levi shakes his head again. "You've got it all wrong. It isn't like that."

"Really, cowboy? Then tell me how it is." I raise an eyebrow, scowling a little for effect.

"Hey, I told you I was going the business route, which is true. You never asked me for more specifics. It didn't seem important to mention my grandfather."

"It didn't seem important that you're practically my landlord? Really?" In my head, I'm thinking of all the potential lease violations that could be brought up and all the things I probably wouldn't have said or done if I'd known my landlord's grandson was living on the other side of the paper-thin walls.

Levi shrugs. "Like I said, I didn't think it was important. I told you I'm here to spend time with my grandpa and to consider the business route, all of which is true."

"Not important that the landlord's grandson lives next door? Not important that I broke into his house and saw him naked? Come on." I exhale, shaking my head at the embarrassing thought.

"Listen, Jodie. Seriously. Yes, my grandpa owns this place. But I'm not here to spy. I'm a tenant just like you. My grandpa's getting older and needs someone to train to take over this place. He owns quite a few rental properties in Ocean City. He wants to show me the ropes this summer so he can retire, and no one else in the family wanted to take over. With my whole bronc riding career down the tubes,

I was sort of out of career options. This just seemed to be logical. He gave me this apartment to live in while I learn how everything works. He thought it would be good for me to have the tenant experience so one day, when I'm running this place and the rest of them, I'd understand it inside and out."

"Still sounds like a spy to me," I reply, tapping my foot. Still, the initial shock is wearing off.

"Come on. It's not like that. I mean, do you have an eviction notice on your door?"

"I don't know, secret landlord, do I?" I tease, tapping my foot more dramatically. I'm not mad, and it doesn't seem like that big of a deal—naked part aside. If I were pissed, though, that anger would be melting right now because even if he is the landlord's grandson, he's one of the sexiest almost-landlords I've ever lived by.

Dammit, why does he have to look so amazing in that muscle shirt? Why does that southern drawl have to stir something within? Why can't I just hate his guts and make this all easier?

He steps toward me, and I stand still.

"No, there's not an eviction notice. Do you think I'd let you go over some stupid party your roommate had? First, it's not your fault. And second, I'm not a saint. I'm flattered that you think I stand on such high moral ground, but in truth, I've had my share of raucous fun. I'm sure as hell not going to hold it against anyone else."

"Really? You were a wild partier back home?" I ask, curious now.

"I've had my fun, believe me."

"What, tipping cows?"

"Okay, that is a bit of a stereotype. But, in fairness, yes, I have tipped some cows among other things." He readjusts his hat.

I grin, shaking my head. "You rebel. Have you ever broken the law?"

"Hold up, I thought we were talking about how pissed you are over my grandpa being the landlord?"

"We are. But now I'm curious," I say, my hand slipping from my hip.

"I mean, there were a few rounds of alcohol when I wasn't quite twenty-one. The typical thing. And maybe an incident with a stolen horse. But listen, in all seriousness, I wouldn't turn you in, Grandpa as the landlord or not."

I ponder this, wondering if I can trust him—and wanting to ask about the stolen horse. I decide, however, to let that one go for now and move on. "Well, if you didn't come over to evict me, what did you come over for?" I ask, staring at him.

"Wanted to see if you needed help with anything, if there were any repairs from yesterday. It sounded like things got pretty wild, so I thought you might need some help."

I bite my lip, weighing my words and the situation. "Are you helping as a friend or as my landlord?"

"I'm not the landlord yet."

"Well, when you do become landlord, how about you at least think about lowering my rent, okay?" I tease, softening.

"I'll think about it. But come on. What can I help with?

I know damn well that Adam Levine poster is covering some damage." He motions toward the poster.

I grin. "What gave it away?"

"Gee, I don't know, the fact that it is randomly placed about a foot from the floor in the weirdest position possible? Come on, let me have a look and then I'll get my tools."

"You don't want to use the purple ones again?" I ask.

"Get real," he says, ripping down Adam and shaking his head as he appraises the huge hole in the wall. "Well, this won't be too bad. It'll take some time, though. What else?"

I sheepishly point toward the refrigerator and the duct-taped handle. He looks at it and then at me. "Tell me this was Gemma's doing and not yours."

"What's wrong with duct tape?" I ask.

"Everything." He sighs and shakes his head. "I'll be right back with the tools. Free of charge. A spy would probably charge, just to be clear."

"No, a spy wouldn't charge to throw me off the trail."

"Okay, Miss CIA. Tell you what," he says. He reaches into his back pocket and pulls out his wallet. "Order us a pizza because I'm starving and, contrary to popular belief, don't have time to make a fire today to cook over. We'll eat pizza, I'll fix this for you, and then I'm headed to meet my grandfather to get some quotes on some repairs at another property."

I look at him, his brown eyes drawing me in. "I don't need your money. I'll pay. After all, you're fixing this place up. Well, even though it technically is your place...."

He shoves the money at me. "Come on, take it. Besides,

I can have it tacked on to your rent if I really want to."

I scowl at him, shaking my head. "Are you always so smug?"

"Are you always this suspicious?"

"Only of you," I say, before spinning to head to the kitchen and grab my cell phone, the twenty-dollar bill in my hand.

"Good. I like that you're keeping an eye on me," he says, strolling out the door to get his tools as I order the pizza, actually feeling a little silly that I thought Levi would really try to get me evicted.

Chapter Eight

Gemma's finally taken my advice. Who knew the girl actually could follow directions? She's gone out to a club tonight instead of partying like a maniac here. Which means I have the place to myself. I don't remember the Home Depot guy's name, but I adore him. He's keeping her all sorts of occupied, which means he's keeping her all sorts of out of the apartment.

I'm almost done with my manuscript edits, but I'm feeling a little low on creative juices. I've only got a few more weeks until this manuscript has to be turned in, and I'm trying not to panic. I've decided to do a little bit of what I call writing research. Which means I'll be watching the scariest horror movies I know, eating some mint chocolate chip, and snuggling under my favorite blanket.

Research doesn't have to be boring, right?

Avery's out on a hot date with Jesse. Knowing those two and their newfound adventurous spirit, they're probably off deep-sea diving or flying to Tahiti or something.

Snuggled up, Sebastian by my side, I hit play on the first movie, all the lights in the house out, the darkness seeping in. I feel the adrenaline bubble inside, which is exactly what I need.

A half hour in, and I forget about the jump scare. It gets me every time, and a bloodcurdling scream emerges from my own mouth. I cover it, laughing a little to myself, hoping I didn't wake up the whole apartment complex.

What feels like ten seconds later, there's a pounding at my door, which causes me to jump and emit a little scream again.

"Jodie, are you okay?" a rugged, panicked voice asks. I shake my head and smile. Of course he would come running to the rescue.

I think about ignoring him, but he'll probably kick in the door and bring a SWAT team in. Guess I better just get up and deal with it.

I'm wearing my "Got Vodka?" pajamas this time around, which are a little less see-through than the margarita glass ones. Nevertheless, Levi's going to start thinking I have a drinking problem.

I trudge to the door after pausing the movie. I don't bother to flick on a light as I open the door.

Levi's standing there wearing boxer shorts and a T-shirt. "Um, hey?" I say, eyeing him.

"Are you okay? I heard you scream." His face is serious, like he's ready to take on a serial killer. Except he's not even armed. Guess he was just going to tackle the killer with his bare hands.

"Yeah, sorry. Just watching horror movies."

"Alone in the dark?"

"That's the only way to watch them, clearly. But yeah, I forgot about that jump scare."

He rolls his eyes, exasperated. "Jesus, I thought something was wrong. That scream was enough to wake the dead. Shouldn't a horror writer be a little, I don't know, used to scary?"

"Levi Creed, are you calling me a wimp?" I cross my arms over my chest, trying not to think about the fact we're both wearing very little clothing, trying not to let my mind wander in the darkness.

"Maybe. I mean, how scary can a movie be? It's not real."

"What, you're not a fan of horror?"

"Can't say I am."

"Have you even watched any?"

He thinks for a moment. "Not that I can recall."

"You haven't watched a single one?" I ask, surprised.

He looks up to the sky for a moment, lost in thought. "No. Can't say I have. More into action movies, to be honest."

"Oh my God. Who are you? Did you live in a bubble down in Texas? Jesus. Get in here."

And before I can think about it, I'm yanking him inside, forgetting about the whole boxer shorts situation and the vodka pajamas.

I pull him to the couch, and he obliges. I pass him the carton of mint chocolate chip as I scramble to get him a spoon.

And then I go to the main menu, find the opening scene, and hit Play. For the next hour and a half, we sit silently beside each other, Sebastian cuddled up to me, passing the ice cream back and forth.

And when the epic jump scare comes at the end of the movie, the one I remember this time, I laugh hysterically when Levi jumps so hard that he drops the half-empty carton on the floor.

"Shit," he mutters, probably embarrassed about his masculinity not being strong enough to stop him from screaming like a girl.

"You know, I'd think a rugged cowboy would be, I don't know, a little tougher when it comes to horror movies. After all, it's just a movie, right?"

He shakes his head, laughing at himself. He puts the ice-cream carton on the coffee table. "You know what, you're awful. Yanking me in here against my will just so you can scare me and laugh at me. Now how am I supposed to go back over there to my lonely apartment and sleep?"

My chest tightens as I turn to look at him, the darkness of the apartment surrounding us, seemingly drawing us closer.

The word "stay" tries to form on my lips, tries to roll itself right off my tongue. I think about what it would feel like to spend the night in Levi's rugged arms, my face buried in his chest, the sound of his accent as he says my name.

I've been there and done that, though. I'm not going to just throw my heart out to be slaughtered willingly. We're neighbors, and I don't know if one night of fun is worth a lifetime of complications, no matter how much my body is aching right now, no matter how much I want him to throw me on my bed and have hot sex with me. Because I'm thinking the no-strings-attached relationship works best if you're not forced to see the guy every day—and, oh yeah, if he isn't basically your landlord. That sort of complicates things.

"Oh, I think you'll manage," I say, getting up from the sofa and flicking on a light, causing us both to shield our eyes like we're allergic to brightness.

"Thanks for the ice cream and the nightmares," he says, grinning, standing from the couch. "I'm gonna go and struggle to fall asleep now."

"Don't you have some moonshine over there? Sure, that'll help."

He flashes a huge smile. "Dad did teach me well."

"You rebel," I say.

"What, you going to turn me in to the landlord?" He juts his chin out, and I shake my head.

"You ass. Get out of here. I hope you have tons of nightmares."

He grins. "Well, then I'll just have to come back over for comfort. Because this is all your fault, you know."

No. It's all his fault. Why the hell did he have to move in right next door, where the temptation is so strong? Why the hell did he have to be this rugged cowboy with just the perfect amount of wild?

And why the hell do I have to be rational and not just go for it? Last year, I criticized Avery for holding back, yet here I am.

I guess once you get burned, it's not easy to put yourself close to the fire again.

So, as I drift off to sleep a few hours later, I turn over and set my alarm for a painfully early wake-up call. I might not be ready to hop into bed with him just yet—lies, in all honesty—but I guess I can at least test the waters, see how much fun Levi Creed could be.

Chapter Nine

I pound on the door, my bright yellow beach bag on my shoulder. I spent way longer on my outfit this morning than I probably should've, deciding on some denim shorts and a pink tank top. Simple. Not too much effort.

I also spent an hour perfecting my "natural" makeup, trying to make it look like I wasn't trying too hard. The thrills of womanhood. I even shaved my legs for this venture, which is saying something since it was 4:30 a.m.

When no one comes to the door, I almost lose my nerve but decide to knock again. After what feels like an eternity, Levi opens the door. He's in boxers and a T-shirt, rubbing sleep from his groggy eyes. He looks naked without his boots and hat, but then again, I've seen him naked—and it is much more impressive.

"Hey, something wrong?" he asks, blinking.

"Nope."

"Okay…," he says, tilting his head.

"I'm here to take you for a seashell hunt." I push past him, letting myself in as I rustle through my huge beach bag, pulling out a Ziploc bag and shoving it at him. "For your treasures."

He stares at me like I'm speaking another language, his face hazy with sleep. "What the hell time is it?"

"It's 5:05. If you want to get the best shells, which I must say are not as impressive as, say, Caribbean shells, not even close, but still, if you want the best we've got to offer, you have to beat the tourists." I've got my seashell hunting game face on, and I'm ready to nab the best of the best. It's been a while since I've hit the beach this early, but if I'm going to show Levi the experience, I figure we have to do it right.

Levi exhales but manages a smile as he runs a hand through his hair. "Are you always this perky in the morning?"

"No way. But I've had two cups of coffee already, so I'm ready to go. Plus, I haven't been shell hunting in forever."

"So you just got up this morning and said to yourself 'Hey, I'll go wake up Levi at the crack of dawn and make him traipse along the beach at an ungodly hour'?"

"Hey, this is your thank-you. Be appreciative."

"My thank-you?" he asks, taking a step back.

"Yeah. For helping me with the washer. And the repairs. And everything else. I'll have you know, not everyone gets my shell hunting expertise and secrets. You're lucky."

"Lucky, huh? I'll remember never to piss you off if this is your version of a thank-you," he says, and I punch his arm. He puts up his hands in self-defense. "I'm just saying, is all."

"Go get your beach gear on. Come on. It's time you live a little bit. Get back in touch with your outlaw self and do something a little adventurous. Well, as adventurous as shell hunting can possibly be, but still. Go get ready. We've got places to be, things to do, and shells to find."

"If you say so," he says, dragging himself back to his room. Johnny Cash's head is tucked into his wing. Apparently, he's not an early riser. I plop down on the plaid couch that screams bachelor. No woman would ever let that pattern in her home. What's even worse, the fabric is scratchy.

A few moments later, Levi reemerges in actual shorts. He's still wearing the T-shirt and still doesn't quite look awake.

"Okay, let's go," I say, grabbing his hand and yanking him after me. After realizing this may be a bit too intimate, too much too fast, I try to pull my hand away after Levi shuts his door. He pulls my hand back to his, however, intertwining his fingers with mine. He looks at me as if asking if I'm going to pull back, but I just smile, easing into the feel of my hand in his.

It doesn't feel odd like it should. This guy is practically my landlord. And we haven't advanced past the neighbor status—not really.

Still, walking down to the beach, my hand in his, it feels right. It feels easy. We carry on at a slow pace, me rambling about seashells and tides and all sorts of things. Levi doesn't respond, though. Maybe it's his sleepiness, or maybe it's because he doesn't know a damn thing about seashell hunting, but he just stares, grinning.

"What?" I finally ask after we get near the water.

"Nothing. It's just I haven't been on a beach in forever."

"Did you go as a child ever?"

"A few times. Grandpa didn't move here until I was way too cool for seashell hunting."

"Cool?"

"What? Are you doubting my awesome swagger?" he asks as we stand at the water's edge, glimmers of orange just beginning to emerge from the recesses of the horizon.

"Oh, I'm doubting it."

"Well, anyway, I was trying to say, this is nice. Despite the crack of dawn wake-up call, I'm happy you invited me."

"Aren't cowboys early risers?" I ask.

"Not beach bum cowboys," he responds, squeezing my hand. I squeeze it back. "Now, let's go before the tourists get here. I want the best damn seashells the beach has to offer."

***

"I still don't believe you haven't been down here for shells. I mean, you found all the best ones. I think you're a liar," I say, eying up Levi's bag of shells. Compared to mine, he found the treasure chest. My bag has a few sad scalloped shells. His has all the nice, souvenir-shop-worthy ones.

"I'm just skilled, I guess. I really haven't been down here yet."

"Well, you have now."

"I reckon I have."

I spin to look at him, cracking up.

"What?" he asks, carrying his bag of shells as I carry mine. We head down the beach.

"Nothing. It's just, who the hell says reckon?"

"Well, who the hell calls a guy out on the word 'reckon'? There are worse things."

"I suppose," I agree as I seal my bag of shells, squeezing the air out of the Ziploc before I do. I gently toss the bag on the sand to be picked up later.

I stop and stare at the water for a long moment, the sun now in the sky. "It's beautiful," I say, shielding my eyes to get a better look, the waves lapping at our toes. And it *is*. It's something I don't stop to appreciate enough.

Levi stands beside me, and I lean against his shoulder. "It is beautiful," he says.

"Better than Texas?" I ask, eying him.

He doesn't take his eyes off me. "In some ways, I reckon so," he says, grinning, his eyes staring into mine. His face is closer to mine than it's ever been, and in this serious moment I take in his rugged jawline, his perfectly set eyes.

For a moment, my heart stops. I think he's going to lean in and kiss me under this picture-worthy sunrise.

For a moment, I think I desperately want him to.

A family runs down the beach near us, though, children's screams breaking the moment, and I avert my gaze from his, staring at the water instead as I come to my senses.

"Do you work today?" he asks.

"Not until this evening. You?"

"I have a meeting with Grandpa late this afternoon. What

do you say we get ourselves some beach chairs and plant them right here, spend the rest of the morning in the sun?"

"Oh, look at that, folks. He's officially turning into a true beach bum."

"It's just nice being out here, you know?" There's a serious tone to his voice.

"I do. I don't get out here enough. All right, deal." I nod, as if in affirmation that this is a wise choice.

"You're not just agreeing because I'm basically your landlord, are you?"

"Oh, shut up. I'll suck up to you when you're actually the landlord. Until then, you're just an odd neighbor."

"Oh really?"

"Really."

"I'll remember that when I send you your first rent bill as landlord," he says, squeezing my hand, then letting go as we turn to head back for beach supplies.

I scowl as I lean down to claim my bag of shells. He takes off ahead of me, dashing toward the apartment, kicking up sand as he does. "Last one there has to buy the chairs," he shouts over his shoulder.

"Too bad I already have some," I yell back, stumbling in the sand as I try to gain my footing and catch up to him.

"Last one there buys lunch then," he replies, already ahead. I run as fast as I can, the wind in my hair, the huge beach bag holding me back. I toss it in the sand, figuring I'll get it when we come back, laughing like crazy at the sight of Levi dashing away from me, his gait not perfect running form because of his leg but still much faster than me—which isn't saying all that much.

Even with one bad leg, that man is freaking fast, I think. Or, maybe I'm just that out of shape. By the time we get to the apartment, we're both huffing and puffing, gasping for air.

Gemma's on the front lawn on my lounge chair. She looks up from her magazine. "What the hell is wrong with you two?" She shakes her head.

"Sorry, ma'am, but we're gonna need that chair," Levi says, gesturing toward it.

"I'm sitting here. And don't call me ma'am. I'm not that old." Even though she's wearing sunglasses, I can tell she's rolling her eyes as she angrily flips a page in her *Cosmopolitan* magazine.

"Well, miss, then, we're going to need the chair."

She gives us a long look before finally stomping out of it like a five-year-old. "You two are such weirdos. You're perfect for each other."

I roll my eyes, mocking Gemma as she flees into the house and slams the door.

"Well, she isn't the smartest girl, I'll admit, but maybe she does know a thing or two," Levi says as he gathers up the chair. Before I can prod him further or take in what he's just admitted, he says, "Go get your other chair. I'll grab some drinks and meet you on the sand."

I smile and head around back to the storage area for my other lounge chair, giddy at the prospect of spending the day with my toes in the sand and Levi by my side. While I'm back there, I also grab something else that I think he might enjoy—two boogie boards.

***

The sun blazes down on us, and my skin's getting crispy despite the sunscreen I mindlessly slapped on this morning. Sweat beads, even though our toes are in the water, our chairs close enough to the edge to let the water lap up to us.

I've got my bikini on underneath my pink tank top and shorts, but it feels like a risk stripping down. Sitting on the beach with Levi is intimate, but going down to my bikini, which is basically lingerie, is a whole new level.

But I've reconnected with the old, confident Jodie. I can't let Darren ruin me for life, and even if I want to, I don't think I can avoid the facts.

My heart flutters when I'm around Levi. It's not the cheesy, tiny ping you can perhaps ignore. I'm talking uncontrollable, bucking flutters, as if *I'm* a rodeo cowboy and my heart's the out-of-control creature. I can't stop this, so I might as well just go all-in. I may as well ride this wave of fun.

I stand up and peel off my shirt, trying not to think about the fact Levi's eyes are glued to my back. I fling the shirt like I'm doing some sad sand striptease. My tank top lands somewhere behind us.

I turn to him now, waiting for him to do the same, secretly needing to see those killer abs again to remind myself I didn't imagine them.

He grins at me, his eyes tinged with what I think might be lust—or at least I hope so.

But Levi doesn't stand, doesn't take off his shirt despite the fact it's like ninety degrees and the sun has to be baking him in that black T-shirt.

"You can't possibly pretend to be shy, cowboy," I say. "I've been witness to your overly abundant confidence."

It's true. He's confident. He's flirty. He's hardly the type to shy away from being shirtless. But now that I think about it, other than the shower scene, I haven't really seen him without some kind of shirt, even if it's an open plaid shirt. Sure, he walks around with an unbuttoned shirt—but I've never seen him with it completely off other than the whole Sebastian-almost-eating-Johnny-Cash incident. And let me tell you, during that incident, my gaze and mind were pretty much occupied by certain regions not related to shirts.

"I'm fine," he says, turning his head to stare at the beach to the left.

"Come on. It's roasting. I took off mine, now you take off yours," I say, taunting him, kicking a little water up at him.

"It's all good. I'm fine."

I raise an eyebrow. "What is it? Spill."

He sighs, looking off into the distance, taking a sip of the soda he brought with him. Finally, he turns to me, looking up into my face. "The accident. I had quite a few surgeries afterward. Left some nasty scars. Just don't want to scare the beachgoers away. It's easier to keep it covered."

I pause, studying him. He's uncharacteristically serious.

"Oh, stop. So you've got a few scars. It's fine," I gently prod.

Okay, perhaps not the most sensitive response, but it's what I'm thinking. It's crazy to me that Levi would be nervous about a few scars. I mean, I certainly get it. We live in a cruel world. But why let that get you down? Why let that make you feel inferior?

He seems to think for a long moment, staring off into the distance. I can tell his mind is reeling, contemplating. I stay silent, letting him think on it.

My tactic works. He sighs, seems to wrestle with his insecurities one final time, and then leaps up from the chair. "You're right. Fuck it." And with that, his shirt comes off and he tosses it in what I presume is a much better striptease move than I demonstrated.

And yes, I notice, the abs are just as amazing as I remembered. This time, I don't shy away from the view. This time, I step toward him, both of us in the shallow water. I push my sunglasses to the top of my head, wanting to look into his eyes unrestricted.

This time, I'm not thinking about being careful or about not showing him my heart. I'm not thinking about how messy this could get if it doesn't work out, or how many times I've been hurt.

I walk up to him, and I wrap my arms around his waist, my hands gently smoothing over the bumpy scars on his back. I don't take my eyes off his, as he looks down into my face.

"You're perfect," I whisper, meaning it. Because he is. He's perfect to me, inside and out.

Looking into his eyes, I see a strong man who has been

through so much, who still carries his scars, both emotionally and physically. I see a man exuding confidence but who is a little broken inside from what others have thought. I see a man ready to take life by the horns but not quite ready to let go of the past. I see a man who is perfectly imperfect in a way that makes me realize how good we could be together. We've both got stuff to figure out, and we've both got our battle wounds. But standing here, the hot sun beating down on us, the truth becomes much clearer than the murky Atlantic waters.

We fit. We just *fit* together.

And that fit could mean a whole hell of a lot of fun.

Standing in the gentle waves, the seagulls cawing above us, Levi leans down until his lips find mine. We kiss, his arms wrapping around me, his skin touching mine. Everything, everything melts away except the feel of Levi Creed touching me, kissing me, his tongue swirling on mine and generating electricity. If I was hot before, I'm on fire now, even the coolness of the salty water not able to put out the heat.

When we pull back, breathless, neither of us talks, as if we're afraid to break the moment. I feel like if I say anything, this might all disappear.

I don't say a word. I simply turn to face the sea, the empty horizon, Levi and I still entwined together, facing the vastness of the ocean and the vastness of the future with one certainty in place: we've got chemistry.

Oh God, do we have the chemistry.

"You ready to try out these boards?" I ask when the

moment has settled between us, when we've accepted the newfound heat.

"Okay, but I don't want to hear you crying when I'm way better than you," he says, grabbing the bigger of the two boogie boards standing in the sand beside us. He dashes into the waves. I grab mine and follow, shrieking at how cold the water is but super excited to dive right in.

Chapter Ten

I'm floating on air like a schoolgirl when I show up for work that evening. Levi and I spent the morning doing the traditional beach stuff. Sandcastles, jumping in the waves, all that. We ate ice cream from the ice-cream truck for lunch, and fell asleep in the sand for a while.

When we headed to our separate apartments to shower and get ready for work, he kissed me one more time, and I thought I was going to melt on the front lawn.

As I walk through the door of Midsummer Nights, Lysander eyes me suspiciously. "You had sex with him, didn't you?" he asks. A few customers turn to eye me.

"What kind of boss just tosses that question around like that?" I ask, teasing as I approach the bar area where he is, Reed also sitting there.

"The kind who is rooting for his waitress and best friend to get laid by a sexy cowboy, that's who," Reed chimes in for him.

I smile, shaking my head. "Well, sorry to disappoint, boys, but no."

"Okay, the Jodie I know only smiles that big when she's getting some hot action. What the hell is happening to you?"

I eye them, shrugging. "Maybe Jodie's growing up a little, realizing it isn't all about sex."

Lysander and Reed both cough and laugh like that's the craziest thing I've ever said.

"Okay, you're right. But I'm just… enjoying it all."

"Oh, shit. This is serious. Jodie's met her match. Like *the* match." Reed holds up his glass in a mock cheer. "When's the wedding? Because I could go for a fun, beach wedding, you know. Just do not tell me there will be cowboy hats involved. No way."

"Slow down. It's not like that. I'm just having fun. If that means Levi and I have a fling, so be it. We're not going past that, though. We're just two consenting adults having a good time, seeing where this goes. It's casual. Super casual. Less than casual, in fact."

"Does Levi know this? That this is just a fling? Does he feel the same way?" Lysander asks.

"Shouldn't I be clocking in?" I ask, trying to change the subject.

"Forget about it. Joseph will handle things for a few minutes. Now spill," Lysander demands as he organizes some liquor bottles behind the bar.

I slump onto the bar, feeling like I'm on an episode of Dr. Phil. "Look, after the whole Darren thing, I've realized I want to just have fun, no commitments, no worries. It's better that way, you know?"

Reed puts up a hand. "Stop. First of all, that name is forbidden here."

"Okay, okay. But anyway, you know I haven't had the greatest luck with men. I've decided to just go with it, stop worrying about forever and commitment. Levi kissed me today, and it was hot. And yes, we clearly have chemistry. But that's it. Just a fun time. Nothing heavy, nothing serious, and definitely nothing forever."

"Oh, Jodie. It sounds like Avery wore off on you. We finally get one of them to go with the flow and open up, and now look, Lysander, we're back to square one with this one. Why so fearful, Jodie? You're the wild, carefree girl we love. Why are you afraid of just giving in?" Reed asks, putting a hand on mine.

"I'm not afraid. I just want to keep it simple and commitment free. I don't think forever is in the cards for me. Why put pressure on us to box whatever this is in? The kiss was fabulous. I just want to enjoy that feeling and not try to make this into something it's not."

"Oh my God, if he did that to you with a kiss, imagine what's going to happen when you knock boots," Reed adds, grinning.

I raise an eyebrow.

"What? I've always wanted to use that expression, and now it fits." Reed smiles, and I shake my head. "Now, seriously, Jodie. Stop being a wimp. I think the problem is you've always just prided yourself on being the fun-loving, sex-driven Jodie who is only in it for lust. I don't care what you say or how you justify it to yourself, but I do think there's a piece of you that wants more. And I think this guy could be the one to change your mind. Love is scary and sometimes it doesn't work out. But listen, sometimes it does, sometimes it really does. Just try to be open to that possibility." He looks at Lysander now, that look they give each other.

"Okay, that's my cue to get to work. When you two get all lovey-dovey, I know it's only going south from here."

"Oh, you're about to go south. Well, southwestern. And I don't think you're ever coming back," Lysander says, winking.

"Was that supposed to be a creative innuendo? Because if it was, you're losing your touch. Anyway, thanks for the pep talk."

"You know we love you and we're rooting for you. Take things slow if you want to, Jodie. Don't rush in. But also don't purposely hold yourself back, if that makes sense." Lysander puts down the glass he's drying and nods.

I tap my chin with my finger. "No, it really doesn't. But I'll think about what you've said."

"Plus, don't forget, if he does break your heart, Lysander and I will plot wild revenge on him to the point he moves out."

"Not going to work," I say as I lift myself up from the bar and prepare to actually get to work.

"Why not? Do you doubt our powers of vengeance?" Reed asks in what is supposed to be a scary, villainous voice.

"No. But the thing is, he's the landlord's grandson, soon

to be the actual landlord."

"Wait, what?" Lysander asks. Reed rubs his hands together and laughs.

"Oh, this is glorious!" he exclaims. "This sweetens the deal even more. Jodie, if you two have enough fun banging, your rent will go down. Who else gets that kind of deal?"

I exhale, not even bothering coming up with an argument. I know there's no arguing with these two.

"Or you could just move in with him. Save some money now and get away from that god-awful roommate of yours," Lysander chimes in. Once those two get going, they just feed off each other.

"I said I wanted to keep things light," I remind them as I start walking away.

"Moving in is light. Sort of. Besides, let's weigh this carefully. Sexy cowboy that we assume is a wild one in bed, or horrible, partying roommate? Who would you rather live with?"

"Well, Gemma hasn't been too bad lately," I offer.

"You just see the good in people," Lysander replies.

"Truth," I agree, Reed following me to the kitchen as I tie my apron on.

"Plus, it's probably just a matter of time until she pulls something horrible again," Reed says.

"Truth," I agree again, because I was thinking that this morning. "But I can't just move in with Levi. Besides, being neighbors has all the benefits without the risk."

"You know, you may be onto something. Maybe I should just buy a house next to Lysander. Late-night sex will still be on the table, but I won't have to deal with his incessant messiness and habit of leaving empty milk cartons in the fridge. So annoying."

"I heard that," Lysander yells from across the restaurant. I shake my head, wondering how I got wrapped up in a workplace this crazy and nosy. I make sure my pen and tablet are in my apron pocket and get to work waiting tables, thinking all the while about my best friends' advice. Most of all, I'm thinking about Levi, letting myself swoon over our kiss far too much, actually dropping a drink for the first time in a year.

"Don't mind her, she's just in love," Lysander says, apologizing to the table and offering a free round of drinks. He winks at me, and I give him the finger when no one is looking.

Who else can do that to their boss?

Of course, who else gets asked about their sex life by their boss?

I don't know where things are going with Levi, but I do know one thing. I've got to keep him away from these two as long as possible, or who knows what's going to happen.

✳✳✳

An hour later, sweat's dripping down my forehead from constantly dashing around. I run from the kitchen to the tables, delivering food, answering questions, and even giving an elderly couple directions to the nearest attractions.

"Hey, can we get some service over here?" a voice yells from one of the booths, and I smile in recognition.

"You can just serve yourselves. You know where everything is," I yell back.

Avery and Jesse are snuggled up in one side of the booth.

"You know, there are two seats in that booth," I say as I amble over to them, truly happy to see them.

"We just like sitting beside each other," Avery says, snuggling up to Jesse.

I pretend to gag. "Just kidding. Love you two. But aren't you tired of this place?"

"No way. It's Tuesday, anyway," Jesse says. Their Tuesday thing. Okay, so it's pretty cute.

"Anyway, enough about us. Give me details. Reed and Lysander already told me about the kiss."

"News travels fast."

"Come on. You're holding out. You slept with him, didn't you?" Avery asks, giving me a creepy wink.

"Uh, do you want me to head to the bar?" Jesse asks, clearly not sure if he fits in this conversation.

"No worries, Jesse. You can stay. Besides, there's nothing to tell. We didn't have sex," I say, matter-of-factly.

"Are you kidding me? I've seen that body. What the hell are you waiting for?" Avery practically squeals, slamming her hands on the table as if I've just told her I murdered a puppy.

Jesse raises an eyebrow, and Avery grimaces. "Long story."

"I'd imagine," he says, but he shakes his head. "Knowing you two, I don't want to know."

"Probably not," I agree. "But listen, I'm taking it slow.

What's the rush?"

"You mean, you're afraid."

"I didn't say that," I argue, tapping my foot before turning my head to look out the window into the dark night.

"You don't have to. I see it all over you. Levi isn't your typical one-night-stand kind of guy. He isn't your love him and leave him from the club or your party hard, one-time thing. He's more like the guy you could get serious with, and that freaks you out."

"Oh my God, why is everyone playing therapist in here today? Maybe I'm just not into him like that, you know, for the long haul. And maybe he's not into that, either."

Avery shakes her head. "Then you're delusional. I can see it on your face. You're a horrible liar. Look, what do you have to lose?"

"I don't see why this is so important, anyway. Why is everyone so interested?"

"Because we want to see you happy," Avery says seriously. "You deserve it. Aren't you tired of the same games? Aren't you tired of the flings with nothing serious to back them up?"

"I thought I was when I met Darren. I also thought Darren was the real deal. I was wrong. Maybe I'm just meant to be single, you know? It's fun. There's just less risk."

Avery sighs, clearly exasperated. "You're impossible. Well, anyway, the little old couple over there is waiting on you. We'll catch up once this place closes."

I smile. "Okay."

"And Jodie?" Avery says as I walk away. I stop and turn.

"We all love you, single, serious, or just plain wild. Okay?"

"Okay." I nod, knowing she means it and thankful that Avery moved here last year. I honestly don't know what I did without her.

I spend the next couple of hours until closing time taking it all in, psychoanalyzing myself, and wondering why I'm having such a hard time with this.

Why *am* I having such a hard time with this? The old Jodie had no qualms about commitment-free fun.

But maybe Avery's right. Maybe I can't be the one-night stand Jodie forever. Maybe the whole problem is deep down, I desperately want the kind of love Avery has with Jesse, the kind Reed has with Lysander.

And maybe, deep down, I'm terrified it's never, ever going to truly work out for me.

***

"So, the kiss, was it good?" Avery asks later. Midsummer Nights is closed for the evening, but Jesse, Avery, Reed, Lysander, and I are left. We're hastily cleaning up as we chat, Lysander deciding we should hang around for a few drinks to catch up. It's been awhile since we've all been in the same place.

"Come on, Avery. Dumb question. From what you've said, that cowboy's luscious in all the right ways," Lysander says.

"Am I the only one here who hasn't seen this dude naked?" Jesse asks, and we all laugh.

"We haven't… yet. But if that ass is as delicious-looking

as Avery says...."

"Reed," Avery scolds, looking sheepishly at Jesse.

Jesse smiles, wrapping her in his arms before saying, "I mean, it probably isn't as good as mine, right?"

It's a good thing Jesse's so chill. Then again, maybe Reed, Lysander, and I have just rubbed off on him. A guy's naked ass probably seems tame compared to some of the things we've talked about.

"Of course not," Avery reassures him, giggling as she turns red.

"Okay, well, I'm going to have to be the judge of that," Reed says.

"Hello, you're attached too. I hardly think it's appropriate for you to be discussing another man's ass, either," I say, shaking my head.

"Oh, it's fine," Lysander says. "We're secure in our relationship. Look, don't touch, that's what we always say."

"Cheers to that," Reed says. "Now anyway, who better to be the judge of men's asses than us? Right? We've got an eye for this sort of thing."

I laugh. "You two are impossible. But I'll be the first to admit, Levi's ass is pretty delicious-looking."

There are squeals and "oh mys" from the group, even Jesse joining in. I immediately regret my confession, and am about to say so when I realize they're all frozen.

And what's more frightening is that they're quiet, the smiles melting off their faces as they eye something behind me.

I shake my head in confusion. "What? Are you really surprised? I can't say his ass looks delicious even though you guys just spent ten minutes talking about it?"

Avery coughs, fixing her hair and gesturing behind me. I freeze. The place is closed. Who would've wandered through the door? But when I turn around, I gasp in horror.

I guess with all the chaos and the music Lysander has playing, I didn't hear the door. We haven't locked up yet, so anyone could've just wandered in.

And wander in, he did.

Shit. I turn all kinds of shades of embarrassed as I try to figure out how to back out of this one.

"I've been called a lot of things," Levi says, approaching us with a grin. "But a delicious ass is not one of them. Thank you. I think."

I cough, wanting to die and sink right into the floor. Avery laughs hysterically.

Reed asks, "It's him, isn't it?"

"Yes," I say. "This is Levi Creed, everyone," I manage. "But we're closed."

"Oh, stop. We're closed to the public. I do believe after the comments he's just heard you make, he is much, much more than just an average customer. Come on in. I was just getting everyone a round of drinks. Have a seat," Lysander says, gesturing toward an empty chair around the table. He rushes to the bar.

"I don't know, I think luscious is a better descriptor in this case," Reed whispers way too loudly, and Levi shakes his head and blushes. Then, apparently emboldened by the scene, shrugs, turns around, and gives us a full view of the buns in their glory before planting them in a seat.

I find myself squealing with laughter, not expecting this side of Levi. Of course, the only side I've really known so far is the neighborly side. Perhaps there's a lot more wild hiding under that hat than I thought.

My friends roar with laughter.

"He's a winner in my book," Reed says, rushing over to shake his hand.

"Hands to yourself, darling," Lysander orders, unloading his tray of drinks as he returns. Reed gives him a look that says "we'll see."

"So, did you come for a drink?" I ask Levi, trying to change the subject.

"Yeah. Plus, I figured I might as well check this place out. I didn't realize the hours."

"Oh, sure. You're here for the food and drinks, huh? Nothing to do with a sexy waitress you might know here?" Avery asks.

Oh my God. This is it. This is where he runs away and says I'm not worth it.

But he doesn't. He just laughs. "Something like that."

This wasn't how I planned on him meeting my friends. All together, they can be a bit much. But, I guess I might as well test the water, right? Jump on in, see if he fits in my life? It's not like there's anything to lose.

Carefree fun. That's what this is. There's no risk.

And within ten minutes, I know he does fit with my friends. He fits right in. He's chatting classic cars with Jesse and answering questions about Texan fashion and style with Reed. He's telling Avery all about his family life—how he's got a brother, how his parents own a small law firm in Texas, and how he grew up. He's fitting in like he's been in this group for years, and I start to see that yes, this could indeed work out.

When Lysander changes the song on the dusty, neglected jukebox in the corner, Levi shakes his head at the pop song blaring.

"This isn't going to work," he says, sighing as he stands and trudges over to the corner. He pops in a few quarters, and a few minutes later some country music is blaring.

Johnny Cash, of course.

I groan.

"Uh-oh. You do know Jodie hates country music, right?" Avery asks.

Levi smiles from the center of the restaurant. He shrugs. "Maybe she'll learn to love it, what do you think? The heart can change, after all."

"God, I'll drink to that," Avery says, holding her glass up. "It wasn't that long ago that someone in this room was telling me to live it up and be open to new experiences. Maybe she should take her own advice."

All eyes are on me, now, wondering what I'll do. "You know, maybe I'll drink to that, too." I take another sip of my beer before dashing out to where Levi is.

I take one of his hands and twirl myself.

"That's what you think a country dance looks like? You have a lot to learn," he says, twirling me anyway, his hands feeling amazing on mine.

"Well, cowboy, I reckon I've never danced to country,"

I say in my best impression of Levi's accent—which isn't very good, in fairness.

"Then let me show you how it's done."

And for the next half hour, Levi shows me the two-step and all sorts of honky-tonk line dances, the rest of the crew eventually joining in. Jesse breaks into some kind of sad kick line with Reed and Lysander, and we are definitely not doing the country music community proud.

But by the end of it, we're all laughing hysterically, sweating from our dancing efforts and drinking, and swearing we're going to have another go at the whole country dancing thing.

"Bring that man back," Lysander says to me as Jesse and Levi talk in the corner about going to some classic car show in a few weekends.

"Screw that, marry that man tomorrow," Reed says.

"How about we start with you getting into bed with that man," Avery says.

I raise an eyebrow. "Avery, someone has loosened up over the past year, huh?"

We all laugh as Avery hits me. I mock her a little, impersonating Avery Johannas of last summer, the whole "I don't want a man," "I don't have one-night stands," girl. I tie it in with a version of the "Look at Me, I'm Sandra Dee" song from *Grease*, and before I know it, she's chasing me around Midsummer, chairs falling, Lysander chanting "catfight" as he pounds on the table with his fist excitedly.

But after we're both out of breath—which doesn't take long since neither of us has kept up with beach yoga or exercise in any form—we hug it out.

"Look, I'm happy for you, seriously. Take it at your own pace," Avery says.

"And I'm happy for you."

"And I'm happy for us all. Now let's get home, huh? I have work in the morning," Jesse says, wrapping his arms around my neck and Avery's.

We all file out, Lysander saying he'll put the place back in order tomorrow morning before the breakfast crowd. Levi and I walk home hand in hand.

"Your friends are pretty awesome," Levi says. "They remind me of my group back home."

"Really?"

"Yeah, sort of. I can see they really care about you, about each other. I've missed that, being here."

"Trust me, I think after tonight, they care about you too."

He pulls me in for a hug when we get to the apartment. "I had a great time tonight. When I moved here, I was unsure of everything. I didn't want to leave home and couldn't see myself being happy here. But Jodie, I am. I really am. Thank you."

I smile as he leans down and kisses me, taking my breath away. When we finally pull our lips apart, I look up into his dark eyes and say, "This rodeo's just getting started, you know? I think we can have fun together."

"Yeah, I'm seeing that. Pure, simple fun." Emphasis falls on the last word.

I look up into his face and smile, realizing we're on the same page. This is a good thing, right? He's just looking for fun, too. I breathe a sigh of relief. This makes it easier. No commitments, no worries about things getting too serious. Just two twentysomething neighbors with chemistry having a good time. Regardless what Avery, Lysander, and Reed think, it sounds perfect to me. It sounds like exactly what I need.

I can handle this. There's no risk in this.

"Right. Just fun," I say with conviction.

As he heads to his door, he turns. "Oh, and Jodie?"

"Yeah?"

"We need to go shopping again."

"For what?" I ask.

"Listen, if I'm going to teach you how to dance country, you at least need a pair of boots." He grins, staring at me as if daring me to defy his observation.

I roll my eyes. "That's not really my thing."

"And board shorts are mine? Come on. It'll be fun."

I picture myself in Daisy Dukes, cowboy boots, and a plaid shirt. It's terrifying. But looking at Levi, thinking about it all, I shrug. "What the hell. Fine. But don't think for a second you're going to make me fall in love with country or start wearing a cowgirl hat, okay?"

"Wouldn't dream of it. Good night, neighbor."

"Good night, neighbor."

He heads inside without looking back, leaving me on the front lawn, staring at the door and then at the starry sky, thinking that Levi Creed still might prove to be trouble… but I think he's going to be a whole lot of fun along the way, if nothing else.

Chapter Eleven

My hot pink cowgirl boots sink into the sand, and I'm pretty sure my feet are drowning in sweat. I don't know how Levi Creed wears boots like these every single day. I miss my flip-flops.

"Okay, I feel ridiculous," I mutter, shaking my head. I'm sporting some tiny shorts and a T-shirt—and the boots Levi insisted I buy. I refused to go all-in with a hat, but I thought maybe I could work these.

But now, these are definitely not working.

"They look good on you. You'd fit right in back home," Levi says, holding the kite in one hand and my hand in the other. He's in his signature jeans and boots, a muscle tank replacing his usual plaid shirt. We look like a mishmash of honky-tonk and beach.

Somehow, though, we're making it work. Sort of.

The wind slaps into my face, the salty air whipping the kite in Levi's hand.

"So, what's the trick?" he asks.

"Haven't you ever flown a kite?" I inquire.

"Of course I've flown a kite. Just not seaside. What's the technique?"

"To hell if I know. I just run like crazy and hope it works."

"Why doesn't that surprise me? You want to be my runner then?"

"Yee-haw."

"Okay, that didn't warrant a yee-haw," he says, groaning.

"Hey, what can I say? The boots are winning me over." I laugh, sprinting down the beach with the sad little diamond kite in one hand, fighting the wind. The beach is pretty barren today, some foreboding clouds spreading over Ocean City. On the way back from our impromptu cowgirl shopping trip, though, Levi had spotted the kite store and insisted we pop in.

I run down the sand clumsily in my boots, thinking about how much fun today has been. The spontaneous Jodie is back, thanks to Levi. I'm the girl who puts the writing aside and just goes exploring, who isn't afraid to laugh and enjoy and just have fun. He may not know the Ocean City ways just yet, but he's learning. And most of all, he's definitely got that free side I absolutely adore.

When I've run far enough, I turn around and run backward, yelling, "Ready?"

"You bet," he yells, and, as the perfect gust of wind comes along, I let the kite go.

It sails up, up, and Levi expertly lets out the string, running back to get it some lift. I look up, staring at the tiny purple kite—I'd insisted on a sparkly one, to Levi's chagrin—as it floats perfectly in the dark sky.

I dash down the beach toward Levi. "It's cute up there," I say.

"I was hoping for a manlier kite-flying experience, but okay," he says, handing me the spool.

I take it, fighting against the wind to hold on to it. Levi wraps his arms around me, and we stare wordlessly at the little kite flying in the great big sky.

Levi kisses my cheek, and I feel like I'm flying right up there too.

"So," he whispers in my ear, "how do you like playing beach cowgirl?"

I grin. "How do you like playing beach cowboy?"

"As long as I have a partner for this strange line dance, that's all that matters."

I turn to look at him, our noses touching. "I have no freaking clue what that's supposed to mean, but I'll assume it means you think we're good together, so I'll take it."

We spend the next ten minutes watching our kite flip around violently in the increasing winds before we reel it back in.

As we're walking back to the apartment complex, the rain starts to fall, and we run toward shelter. I dash toward my door, but Levi pulls me back.

Just like some crazy romantic movie, he yanks me into him, the rain now beating down like only seaside storms can. He takes my mouth with his, devouring me in a kiss I'm sure would steam up windows. His tongue finds mine and swirls expertly, telling me he's kissed plenty of girls. He's experienced, and he knows exactly how to make me breathless. I savor every second of the kiss, his hands finding my waist and pulling me to him, his strong body inviting me in.

I've kissed enough guys to know kisses like these are on their own level.

When he pulls back, he says, "I have to go away for a few days. My grandpa wants to take me along for a meeting with a contractor for some repairs on the Fenwick Island property he owns. Do you want to come, slip away for a few days? You can bring your writing."

I peer into his brown eyes, thinking about how nice it would be to escape from Gemma and from all the daily realities. But then I sigh, coming to my senses.

"I can't. I have work at Midsummer Nights."

"I'm sure Lysander would let you slip away for a few days," he argues, kissing my neck in exactly the right spot.

I bite my lip, thinking about it, the carefree side of me wanting to say yes.

Drowsy and dazed from the kiss, I want to run off with him on a crazy road trip, if for nothing else than for the chance to kiss him some more. But then I stop, thinking about what a trip like this could mean. I think about all the reasons this could be a bad idea.

So, the side of me that usually doesn't surface comes to the light—the rational side. The careful, cautious side.

"I think I better sit this one out. But rain check?"

Levi grins, looking up at the sky. "Rain check."

He kisses me one more time before we part ways. As I hop in the shower before heading to work, I find myself thinking about that kiss, wondering what it would be like to be kissing him here under the shower head, his hands all over my soapy body....

How the hell did this happen? I wonder. *How the hell did I fall so damn hard for a semitamed cowboy next door? And how the hell do I keep from getting ahead of myself?*

Because the more I'm around him, the more I'm sure this isn't going to be a slow, practical ride. It's going to be the wildest ride ever... and inside, I tingle at the mere thought of it.

***

I walk through Midsummer Nights with a smile on my face. Lysander is in the corner, yelling at Reed as he hangs up some new Shakespearean beach art that they had commissioned from Avery. It's pretty sweet, a hip Shakespeare standing at a tiki bar, the ocean waves in the background.

"A little more to the left," Lysander barks. Reed turns and stares at him.

"Are you serious? You just told me a little to the right a minute ago."

"Well, then you went too far."

I wander up behind them, leaning over Lysander's shoulder. "You two are like a damn married couple."

"Well, in that case, we give marriage a bad name, because I'm going to murder him before the night's over," Reed says, still holding the picture up. I take the other side and help.

Midsummer Nights is packed with the Thursday night regulars, but Joseph and the new waitress, Maria, are working. Maria's a natural, Avery having helped train her. Lysander had to hire some new help with Avery's painting business pulling her away so much.

Reed looks at me, shaking his head. "You fool."

"What?" I wonder if I'm holding the painting wrong or something. He shakes his head.

"You didn't sleep with him yet."

"Okay, one, how do you know?" I raise an eyebrow.

"I just know. Body language. You've got this sexual tension."

"Oh my God, you creep. You can't just say that," I say, hitting him with one hand. The painting slides down a little, and Lysander gasps.

"Will you two focus?"

"Sorry," Reed and I mutter at the same moment.

We go through a series of moving the painting around—up, down, up again, left, left more—and finally, Lysander is happy with where it is.

"Now just don't move while I climb up and put a nail in."

While we're waiting, Reed turns to me. "So, you really didn't, did you?"

"Oh my God, no. I did not sleep with my *neighbor*."

"But you want to?"

I roll my eyes before my grin becomes too big to hide. "Okay, you've got me. Of course I want to. Have you seen him? He's gorgeous. And it's been… well, too long. I just…. Levi's different."

Reed smiles and winks. "Like, kinky shit different, or like, mama's boy, I only have sex when I'm married different?"

"You are unbelievable," I say, feeling myself blush as Lysander climbs up to put the nail in the wall.

"Hey, I'm just trying to sort this all out."

"Did it ever occur to you that I can sort out my own sex life?" I ask, shaking my head.

"Well, what's the fun in that?" Reed asks.

Once we're finished, I bolt to the back as fast as possible, hurrying to busy myself with tables.

An hour into my shift, Jesse Pearce walks through the door and grabs his usual Tuesday night booth. I sidle over, confused.

"It's not Tuesday, you know. And where's your better half?"

Jesse smiles, but I can tell he's a little off.

"Everything okay?" I ask, concerned by the tension apparent on his face.

He nods. "Yeah, yeah. Just… I was hoping I could chat with you a few minutes."

"Oh shit, did Reed put you up to this? Because I'm not answering any more sex-life questions." I turn to see Reed smiling from the bar.

"Don't you have a business to run?" I yell over to him, referring to his boardwalk souvenir shop, Sand Dollars. It's a running joke that Reed probably doesn't even know what his shop looks like because he's basically never there. Luckily, he hired some top-notch clerks to work there and manage it. At this point, I think they're more like owners than Reed.

"That's why you hire people, so you don't have to," he replies, turning to eye Lysander.

"I assure you, this has nothing to do with your sex life or Reed. I don't even want to ask at this point. But I have something else to ask. Do you have a minute?"

I sigh, eying the restaurant. Looks like Joseph and Maria have it together.

"Sure," I say, sitting across from him. Looks like I'm doing a stellar job at working hard today.

"I have a favor to ask."

"Okay," I say, wondering what Jesse could possibly need but willing to help.

Jesse reaches into his pocket and pulls out a jewelry box, sliding it across the table at me. I open it to find a sparkling blue diamond that is big and beautiful.

"Jesse, I'm flattered. But I'm going to have to say no," I tease, smiling.

He shakes his head, taking the box from me to examine the ring.

"It's gorgeous. I'm so damn excited," I squeal, which causes Lysander and Reed to rush over.

"Oh my God, you two are like a swarm of bees," I say.

"I heard you squeal and saw a sparkly diamond from across the room. Of course we're over here," Lysander says, smiling. "Is this what I think it is?"

Jesse blushes. "Yes. And actually, I could use all of you if you're willing to help. I just—I want this to be special for Avery. And to be honest, I'm nervous as hell she's going to say no, with everything in her past. I want this to be intimate and beautiful. I want her to know it's different this time."

"What do you have in mind? How can we help?" I ask.

"Okay, here's my plan," Jesse begins, and we all hover around him like he's about to give us battle plans. "I'm hoping, Lysander, you could let me borrow this place on a Tuesday night. Like, clear it out. I'll tell Avery I wanted us to have a romantic night out since we've both been busy. I'll get her here under the ruse we're just having our Tuesday dinner."

"That's easy. No worries. Reed and I will even have a beautiful meal ready for you," Lysander says.

"I was hoping you could keep it simple. Burgers and fried pickles, like the first night we talked here."

"You've got it. That's adorable," Reed says, the excitement evident in his voice.

"Okay. Jodie, here's where you come in. I'm thinking about a half hour later, I'm going to pop the question. But you know how Avery loves Henry, and I want him to be a part of it. Jake, too. I was wondering if you could bring Henry and Jake by when I drop you a text. I'm going to have a little backpack for each of them. Jake's backpack is going to have a note that says, 'Will you' inside and Henry's will have a note that says, 'Marry Me' and the ring. You just have to sneak them in the back and let Jake come in first. Henry comes in a moment later. I'll take care of the rest."

"Oh my God, that's adorable," I say. "Of course I can be the dog handler for the night. Yes!"

"You guys don't think it's cheesy?" Jesse asks, worried.

"I think it's cheesy as hell, which is exactly why it's perfect. You need it to be cheesy romantic," Reed says.

Jesse smiles, seemingly feeling better after getting the Reed stamp of approval.

"Do you think she's going to say yes?" he asks, turning to me now.

I give him the widest grin. "Are you kidding? I think she's going to jump in your arms and ask you to marry her right then."

"I don't know. I just…. With the past…." It's obvious Jesse's spent a lot of time in his head over this. I get it, though. I can't blame the guy for panicking, with Avery's ex being such an ass and the marriage ending on such a bad note—as in a young, perky blonde in Avery's bed with her husband bad. It sort of leaves a jaded image of marriage in one's head, I'd imagine.

I smile assuredly at Jesse, though. "The past is done, and she's over it. You two have been living together for a while now, and it's going so well. I've never seen her so happy. She loves you. She loves you because you've shown her the past doesn't have to be the future. Just be confident. She's not the same Avery she was with him. Hell, she's not the same Avery who first came to Ocean City. She's a different, better version of herself because of you. I think she's figured out that love with you is different—a good different."

"Okay." He exhales, nodding, his green eyes seeming to

soften in relief.

"So, when is this happening?" I ask, needing to know the practicalities of it all now.

"I'm thinking this Tuesday, if it's possible? It's the anniversary of our first kiss."

"Oh my God, that's adorable," I say, swooning over the thought.

"Can you get a new word? I think you've said 'adorable' like ten times," Lysander says, poking me.

I roll my eyes.

"I'm grabbing drinks for us. This calls for a celebration," Lysander offers.

"She hasn't said yes *yet*," Reed argues, following him.

"How long until it's their turn?" Jesse asks, motioning toward Reed and Lysander.

I smile. "They already act like a married couple. But God bless us because I feel like their wedding isn't going to be low-key in the slightest. There will be a month-long fight over every single aspect."

"You're right," he says, laughing.

"Seriously, Jesse. I'm happy for you guys," I say, turning the conversation back to the exciting news.

"Thanks. Thanks for everything. If it weren't for you.…"

I nod. "Yeah, I'm a hell of a matchmaker."

Jesse starts to talk, and then stops himself.

I scowl. "What? Go on. What were you going to say?"

"I was going to say that for a hell of a matchmaker, you sure take your sweet time recognizing when your perfect match is right next door."

"Oh no. Not you, too." I bury my head in my arms on the table, groaning.

I only pick my head up when I hear Lysander trudge back to the table. He's got a round of Love-in-Idleness drinks.

"To the soon-to-be happily married couple," Lysander says as we clink glasses.

"And to the soon-to-be bedded Jodie and her cowboy," Reed adds in, just to stir me up.

Instead of letting him get to me, I just laugh. "I'll drink to that," I say, staring defiantly at Reed. I've finally shut them up, I realize, as I wink at them and down my drink.

Chapter Twelve

"Oh my God, you were right. It was just a matter of time. Gemma's back to her craziness again, and I swear, I'm going to lose it," I bellow into the phone from my room, the music blaring. Sebastian is curled up on my bed, restlessly flopping as I hear someone yell "shots" from the living room. It's Saturday night, and I should be sleeping or working on my edits. Instead, I came home to a party zone that is just out of control.

"Jodie? Is that you? What in the hell is going on? Are you at the club without us?" Lysander asks.

"I'm at home. I came home from work to find this crazy-ass party. Gemma has like ten people over, mostly guys. Apparently, the Home Depot guy dumped her, so this is her way of comforting herself. There's a whole lot of ridiculousness happening, not to mention a whole lot more twerking than I've ever needed to see. I need to get work done. I'm working on round two of edits, but this is just nuts. I can't leave, either, because who knows what kind of condition the apartment will be in when I come back. I think they've taken the "Shots" song a little too seriously at this point."

"Kick them out," Lysander says practically.

"Tried a few times. There are too many of them."

"Call Levi?" he asks.

"He's out of town." I clutch my head, the bass of the new song giving me an instant migraine.

"Call the cops?"

"On my own apartment? Are you kidding? But I'm afraid if I don't do something, someone else is going to make that call," I say, frustrated. This is ridiculous. How am I in this position again?

"You know what, say no more. Reed and I will be over," Lysander offers.

"And what are you two going to do?"

"Come on, really? You know we've got all kinds of tricks up our sleeves. We'll figure something out."

"That's what I'm afraid of."

The phone clicks, and I shake my head, annoyed that I'm back in the role of Mom or RA in what feels like an out-of-control sorority house. So much for the sweet and innocent act Gemma had going online. This girl is a maniac, and she's got to go.

Contract, lease agreement, or whatever other binding documents aside, I can't take this anymore. Jesus, I need a lawyer.

Or I need about fifty drinks.

But half an hour later, I realize all I really need is Reed

and Lysander because they definitely have a Gemma-party-squashing repertoire up their sleeves.

***

When I get the text to get ready for their entrance, I head to the living room. Gemma is dancing on the couch, screaming and singing in a thong bikini—yes, a thong bikini, not that I wanted to see. About ten drunk college-aged guys and girls dance around her like some weird music video, their drinks sloshing about. I feel like it should be illegal to even watch and, what's worse, I feel super old.

And then the door flies open. "We're here, darling," Reed says.

I've seen Reed and Lysander in all sorts of weird situations. I've been to a Halloween party where they dressed up in some super-scandalous outfits. I've seen all sorts of pranks and gimmicks.

But this wins. This so wins.

My eyes are about to bulge out of my head as they stroll in, both wearing actual purple leisure suits and looking like some sad excuse for Austin Powers. They've got their hair styled like it's the seventies, and Reed is even wearing platform shoes.

It's so awful, I want to cry for them.

Gemma stops her twerking on the sofa, eying them.

"Cut the music," she says, as if this is really a music video. One of her cronies obeys as Reed and Lysander strut forward.

"Darling, what are you doing? Come give your dads

some kisses," Lysander says.

"What the fuck?" she shrieks, looking as confused as she should. "Who the hell are you?"

Reed shakes his head, wagging a finger at her. "Come on, silly girl. It's Pops and Pops. We told you we were flying in."

I shake my head, not believing this is happening. When they said they were going to take care of it, I didn't think they were going to adopt a daughter for a day. My face is burning in humiliation for Gemma as her friends look from the two leisure-suit dudes to Gemma and back again.

"These are your dads?" one of the girls says, raising an eyebrow.

"What? No. I don't know who these weirdos are. Get out, or I'm calling the cops."

This is my cue. I've got to be convincing, although I'm skeptical this ridiculous plan is going to work.

"Gemma, don't be crazy. You told me this morning your dads were coming over. Come on, I made fresh lemonade for us. Will your friends here be joining us?"

"Are you psycho? What the hell is this?" Gemma yells, clearly intoxicated but sober enough to know this is the most ridiculous thing she's ever heard. She leaps down from the couch now, shoving some of her friends to the side.

"Oh, sweet Gemma. You don't have to be embarrassed. We talked about this. Our love life isn't going to bother your friends. Right, guys? Is that what this is about? I'm sure your friends are fine with it, right?" Lysander says.

A few of the guys look like they don't know what to believe. Lysander wanders over, putting an arm around one of the drunk guys' shoulders, rubbing him creepily and leaning in way too close. "This fine man looks like he'd like to have some lemonade with us. You would, right, darling?" Lysander's hand strokes his shoulder, and he's about an inch from the guy's face.

I have to bite my lip to keep from laughing. The guy looks uncomfortable.

"Uh, nice to meet you Mr. and Mr. Rayne, but I've got to get going. Sorry, things were a little crazy here anyway. I told Gemma to settle it down. I'm going now." He scooches out from under Lysander's arm, dashing to the door like a weird high school kid.

"Oh, no, look at this one, Lysander. So adorable. Gemma, you've picked such attractive friends," Reed says, wrapping his arm around another guy's shoulders and squeezing him tightly.

"Dude, what the fuck?" this one yells, slinking out from under Reed's grasp and looking totally confused. He gives Gemma a look before dashing out the door, the party spirit clearly gone.

One by one, the partiers follow, confused by the fact Gemma's dads—the ones she refuses to claim—are here, that they're wearing leisure suits, and that they don't seem to understand personal space. I can't believe it. They're scaring them away. It's working.

Gemma is freaking out, now standing on the floor, begging her friends to stay, that these aren't her dads, that her parents aren't gay, and that her real parents wouldn't be caught dead in those outfits. It doesn't matter, though.

The party vibe is over.

"You're not driving, right?" Lysander asks a few of the clearly intoxicated kids. "Here, let me pay for a cab." He gets on his cell phone and calls the cab company.

"Thanks, sir. I think we'll just wait outside for our ride." The boy doesn't make eye contact.

"You bet." Lysander smiles and nods, Reed winking. The boys exit quickly.

Gemma whines like a five-year-old. "Tony, don't go. This is absurd. This isn't…. You don't understand."

Tony heads out the door as Reed winks at him.

When the party is cleared out, Gemma turns to me, rage in her eyes.

"You freaking psycho. What, you can't stand that I'm young and beautiful and fun? What's wrong with you? Bringing your gay friends in to pretend they're my dads? Are you kidding me? And what the hell are they wearing? Jesus."

Reed says, "Honey, we did you a favor. What good do you think is going to come of all those gross guys here? Any man who is okay with being one of many vying for the same girl isn't any man you want. Trust me. I've been down a similar road. Respect yourself more. It's okay to have fun, but not like this."

It's a sweet sentiment and good advice. "He's right, you know," I say, trying to comfort Gemma. Despite her annoying habits and the fact she's probably going to get me evicted—Levi or not—I feel for her. This girl clearly needs some guidance.

"Fuck you all. Newsflash, but you're not my fathers, you weirdos. I should have you arrested."

She stomps toward her room. I turn to Lysander and Reed, figuring I should just give Gemma space.

I sigh, shaking my head. "You guys *are* kind of weirdos."

"Honey, was it the two dads thing that scared them away?" Lysander asks, smirking.

"I'm pretty sure being gay was the least of their concerns. It could've been the suits. That was enough to scare me. Or maybe it was that you were the creepily sexual parents who seemed to be hitting on everyone in the room. My God, those people are going to have nightmares."

"Hey, did we or did we not clear out the party? Usually I wouldn't be proud of my party clearing skills, but tonight, it worked in our favor."

"Where in God's name did you two get the suits? How the hell do you have them so quickly? Who keeps leisure suits lying around?"

"Too many questions. Just trust us on this one—Lysander and I have quite a repertoire of costumes, if you should ever be in need. Lysander wanted to go for the merman outfits we had, but even I thought that might be too much. I thought stuck-in-the-1970s dads who were gay and overly touchy-feely would do the trick. Those college boys think they're tough. Please. Such wimps. A little purple suit scares the shit out of them. Unreal."

"You two are unreal, but thank you, I think. Although things with Gemma are definitely going down the tubes after this one," I say, grimacing at the thought of what tomorrow will bring.

"Things were down the tubes before tonight. That girl's terrible. Seriously." Reed waves his hand in the air. I really can't disagree with him.

"Anyway, looks like we've cleared this place out. Guess you can go get your work done now," Lysander says.

I sigh. I really should go finish my edits. Unlike Gemma, I should be responsible.

But I just don't feel like it. I don't want to spend another second in this apartment tonight.

"I don't know if I'm in the writing mood. I think I've just seen too much twerking tonight to write effective horror."

"Oh, thank God. We were hoping you'd say that. I mean, we're already dressed to impress. Might as well make the most of it and go out. Maybe we could take that awful girl with us, show her what fun really looks like."

I toss my hands up. "If you take her, she's your responsibility."

"I've never backed down from a challenge," Lysander says. He heads down the hallway to knock on her door.

"He's crazy," I say, heading to my room to get changed.

When I emerge in a clubbing outfit, Lysander is standing with Reed. "Gemma says she doesn't want to go out. Says she wants to wallow in grief. I offered to stay with her, but she said something like 'fuck off.' So yeah, I think it's good to get out of here."

"Well, her loss. At least we tried. Now let's go. I could go for some fun," I reply.

"A little hypocritical. You did want to shut down

Gemma's party so you could work," Lysander observes. Reed hits him.

"Don't dissuade her. She's actually going out."

"He's sort of right. Am I awful?" I ask, worried.

"No, of course not," Reed says.

I feel a pang of guilt. I didn't mean to embarrass Gemma. I could've probably handled things better, but it's too late now.

So, after shrugging it off, I say, "Oh well. Let's go. Marooned Pirate?"

"No way, honey. In these suits, I've got the perfect place."

"Oh yeah?" I ask, and then I smile in acknowledgment.

"Gino's," we all say at the same time. It's the only gay bar in town, and it's got a funky 1970s vibe.

"Yeah, those outfits look like they were made for Gino's."

"Let's go, girlfriend. All the fun of going out without worrying about any man trying to steal you from the cowboy." Lysander winks.

It sounds wonderful to me as we head out, leaving behind the drama that has become my apartment life.

Chapter Thirteen

We don't stay out too late. A girl can't go clubbing too often, after all. It starts to wear on you.

I return home before midnight, deciding to do some writing. I end up falling asleep with my laptop on my bed, waking up to the sun streaming in.

When I meander to the kitchen, not feeling too bad since I only had one—I know! One! —drink last night, I notice the kitchen and living room are empty. That's strange. Gemma's usually up and clanging around by this time.

Mostly out of curiosity and partially out of a need to set things right, I amble down the hallway toward Gemma's room.

The door is wide open. Gemma's dressed—and packing.

"What's going on?" I ask, confused. Maybe she's got a business trip or something.

Gemma looks up at me, anger in her eyes. "Really? You have to ask? What's it look like?"

I shake my head. "I don't know. Look, I know last night was crazy, but you have to admit, you said you weren't going to throw any more parties."

"You know what's crazy?" she asks, stopping her shoving of clothes in boxes to walk toward me, pointing a finger like I'm a child being lectured. I feel put on the defensive. "You. You expect me to live here and be your perfect little roommate like Avery. Newsflash. I'm not freaking thirty. I'm not some washed-up, boring writer like you. I like to have fun. I thought living by the beach would be a blast, but it turns out you're a weird, psychotic drag with creepy friends. I'm done. I don't care about the lease. I don't care about the contract. I'm out. Goodbye. It hasn't really been fun."

I'm speechless. I'm shocked. I'm a little hurt, actually.

And I'm also a little relieved. Let's face it. This whole roommate thing hasn't been working out.

"You know, maybe we're just at different stages of life. A while ago, I'd have been partying right there with you. But people change. I've grown up a bit. This just isn't working, so I agree. It's time for us to part ways."

"Oh, how philosophical of you. I knew Craigslist was the worst idea ever."

"Look, I'm sorry. Do you want help?"

"I'm fine. Thanks, but no thanks." She angrily tosses a few more things into her suitcase, her scowling face clenched with rage.

I raise my hands, stepping back. Apparently, I can't do anything to fix this.

I'm not going to lie, a big part of me sighs in relief as I head to the kitchen for a cup of coffee.

Another part of me panics a bit. Because with Gemma moving out, I'm back to square one with the financial situation.

Shit.

Not time to worry about it, though. I've got to be at work.

So, for now, I'll just wave to Gemma after the last box is loaded and kiss this chapter of life goodbye.

And I'll remind myself to never, ever look online for a roommate again. Avery was apparently a diamond in a sea of rocks. I'll count my blessings, count my pennies, and figure something out.

* * *

A few mornings later, there's a knock at the door. Gemma's completely moved out, not a goodbye hug or anything—not that I'm surprised or even sad about that—but I wonder if it could be her, returning for a forgotten item.

God, I hope not. I stumble to the door in my pajamas and find Levi.

I smile, not even worrying about how rough my hair probably looks. "Hey, how are you?"

He hands me a coffee from the shop down the street. I usher him in.

"Do you have to work?" he asks.

"Nope. But I do have a job tonight. Jesse needs my help proposing to Avery." I squeal and do a little happy dance.

Levi eyes me. "Well, that was interesting."

"Look, I helped match them up. It's just exciting to see my hard work and matchmaking skills pay off."

"So, you're into the whole fairy-tale wedding scene, huh?" he asks.

"Um, not for me. I think weddings are a bit overrated. At least the whole expensive limo, ridiculous flowers, thousands of dollars on a dress weddings. I mean, I don't think it has to be over the top. And personally, I don't even know if I believe in marriage. Didn't work out for my mom, and I haven't seen it work out very well for anyone else. Still, if this is what Avery and Jesse want, I'm thrilled for them. If anyone can make it work, it's them."

"I hear you. Although my parents have made it work, I don't know. Then again, I've got a jaded opinion of love."

I take a seat at the island, warming my hands on my coffee as I contemplate the question I want to ask. "Does this have to do with the serious relationship you had when the accident happened?"

He sighs. "Wow, welcome back, Levi, let's chat. How was your trip? And let's talk about your lost love that didn't work out."

I wince. "Sorry."

"I'm teasing. Actually, I'm putting off talking about it."

"You don't have to talk about it. Just curious. How was your trip?"

"The trip was boring, actually. Would you believe Grandpa didn't want to get up at 5:30 a.m. to look for shells? Something about business meetings and contractors and boring stuff. But anyway, back to the whole Molly story—that was her name—yeah, my jaded view of love does revert back to her.”

“Were you two engaged?” I guess.

“Bingo.”

“And she left after the accident?”

“Bingo.”

“That’s horrible,” I say, cringing. “What kind of woman would do that?”

“A beautiful one who had a heart of gold. We were crazy about each other. So, it makes me wonder about love at all. If she couldn’t promise to love me forever and mean it, I don’t know who could. I just lost faith in the whole thing, you know? But it’s all good. Like we’ve said, fun is the way to go.”

“To fun,” I say, clinking my coffee cup against his before taking a sip.

“Speaking of fun, where’s Gemma?” he asks, grinning.

“She’s gone.”

“Are you serious?” He leans closer, as if he can’t believe me.

“Yep.”

“Shit, sounds like I missed some fun. What happened?”

“Well, long story short, she had another wild party with a bunch of asshole college kids, and refused to shut it down when I got home. Lysander and Reed showed up in leisure suits, pretended to be Gemma’s fathers, and got super touchy-feely with some of the male partiers. Let’s just say it got uncomfortable really quick, and the party cleared. Gemma got pissed and left for a roommate much cooler than me."

"Wow, that was easy. If you'd known that sooner, right?"

"Don't act so happy. I know you'll miss the free peep show you got when she strutted around here half-naked."

Levi raises an eyebrow. "Okay, let's clarify. First, I'm not peeping in your windows. That's you that sneaks into people's windows. Two, Gemma's not my kind of girl."

I raise an eyebrow in disbelief. "Really? Perky boobs, perfect hair, tight-body girls aren't your thing?"

"No," he says seriously. "Maybe in the past. But no. Girls like Gemma are shallow. I may like fun, and I may like to keep things unattached, but I don't do shallow. Not anymore."

"Interesting. A no-strings-attached guy with principles. I like it." I take another sip of coffee, keeping my gaze on him.

He grins. "You make me sound like a weirdo."

"You are a weirdo. But a good, moral weirdo."

"So, what are you doing before the whole proposal thing?"

"Just doing some writing. Why?"

"Wondered if you want to get breakfast? I want to hear the long version of the Reed and Lysander story because it sounds interesting."

"Oh, it is. I could do breakfast. Let me go get ready." It doesn't take much to get me distracted from my writing these days, which is perhaps why I've had to ask for extensions on my deadlines three times. Oops. But right now, breakfast with Levi seems worth the shirking of my responsibilities.

I smile, heading to my room as Levi talks to Sebastian, who is meowing at his feet.

It's so weird, but it feels natural. Levi here, going to breakfast. It feels like we've been doing this forever.

When I emerge dressed appropriately for breakfast, Levi asks, "What are you going to do about the roommate thing?"

"I have no clue. I'm back to square one. I know I'm not going online, that's for sure."

"I'm sure you'll figure it out," he says, and I nod.

"Somehow I always do. Now, more importantly, we have something else to figure out."

"What's that?" he asks, taking my hand as we stroll out into the sun.

"Where are we going for waffles?"

"Waffles? Pancakes are the best breakfast."

"Oh my God, who are you?" I ask, shaking my head.

"Last I checked, your amazing neighbor who you missed oh-so-much. You're not plotting to scare me away like you did Gemma, are you?"

"Honey, I've been plotting that since the day you moved in."

He sighs. "I kind of thought you were going to say that."

We head off into the muggy August morning, the sticky weather matting my hair to my head as we stroll down the sidewalk toward a local café, chatting about Levi's trip and Gemma's exodus as if we're two close friends being reunited.

Except for the fierce spark I feel as his hand squeezes mine.

***

"Are you sure it's okay if I'm here? I don't want to intrude."

"Hush. Things need to be perfect, and although I assured Jesse I can handle it, maneuvering the two laziest dogs in Ocean City and getting them to cooperate isn't going to be a walk in the park. Now come on. Help me get Jake into his backpack."

I'm out of breath from trudging up the stairs to Jesse and Avery's apartment and from trying to get Henry into his backpack. The two-hundred-pound mastiff refused to get off the couch, so it was quite the dance I had to pull off to get him in his engagement setup.

Jake, who is currently snoring on his side, tongue on the carpet in the living room, doesn't look like he's apt to walk to Midsummer Nights and perform an engagement miracle, either.

"You did put the ring in there?" Levi asks, pointing to Henry's backpack.

"Of course I did," I snap. Levi puts his hands in the air. I sigh. "Sorry for snapping. I'm just stressed."

"Jodie, it's going to be fine. I mean, how hard can this be? We've just got to get the dogs to Midsummer."

"Without anyone seeing us and without Avery hearing us. Oh, and they have to make an entrance on cue," I say, handing Levi the backpack Jake needs to put on, and then scampering off to get the leashes.

"Relax. I handled a crazy-ass horse in the ring. Think I can manage these two," Levi says cockily.

"My, someone is confident. Glad I brought such an

animal expert. If anything goes wrong, I'm blaming you."

He grins. "Wouldn't you blame me anyway?"

I think for a moment. "Yeah, probably. Now let's get moving. We have to be there in fifteen minutes, and with these two being so sluggish, it's going to be like an hour until we get there."

"I've got this," Levi says, heading to the kitchen and rustling through cupboards. He emerges with a bag of potato chips.

"Hey, cowboy, we don't have time for snacks. Get Jake's leash and let's go."

I attach Henry's leash to his collar and tug.

And pull.

And coax him.

And beg him.

And yank with all my might.

He doesn't budge.

Levi chuckles behind me. I'm ready to scream when Levi rattles the chip bag, offering Henry one.

Henry opens his eyes, sees the chip, and is instantly off the couch, drool dripping from his mouth. Jake, hearing Henry snacking, perks up as well.

Levi shoots me an I-told-you-so glance.

"Shut up and let's go," I say grumpily, but internally relieved.

We trudge through the humidity toward Midsummer, Levi enticing the dogs with chips, carrot-in-front-of-a-donkey style. We manage to get to Midsummer, and I sneak us in the back entrance that Lysander left open. I see

Lysander and Reed hiding in the back corner of the kitchen, being quieter than I ever thought possible.

"I didn't think you guys would be here still," I say. Their job was to have dinner ready for Jesse to grab from the back.

"Did you really think we were going to leave without witnessing this? Come on. Now shut up so we can hear," they say, propped against the wall trying to eavesdrop.

There's music playing, and it's basically impossible to hear. Dammit. I wanted to hear the romantic words, too.

We all stand in the middle of the kitchen, trying to keep the dogs still and quiet.

Henry plops down on the kitchen floor, asleep in a second. That was easy. Jake sits, staring at Levi, begging for more potato chips. The bag is almost empty.

"Uh, Avery, wait, I'll get it," we hear a frantic voice say.

"Be right back," she says, and we hear her footsteps coming closer.

Panicked, we all look at each other. "Shit," I mouth, trying to figure out what to do.

Lysander points toward the walk-in freezer. We try to dash for it, but Henry won't budge, not even for a chip. The walk was too much.

We hear Jesse running after her. "Sit down, woman," he says before she makes it to the kitchen. They're standing right at the counter now, the swinging doors to the kitchen the only thing blocking Avery from us.

"Jesse, you're acting freaking weird," she replies, as we stand as still as possible, nobody moving a muscle now, praying Jesse can talk her down and back to the table.

"I just need some hot sauce. It's right back here," she says.

There's a moment of silence, and we all hold our breaths.

"Dammit," Jesse says. "Can't you ever just let me take care of you? Can't you ever just sit back and relax?" There's a lightness to his voice, though. I can tell he's smiling.

"I mean, again, it's just hot sauce," Avery says. "What's wrong with you tonight?"

"I didn't want to do this behind the counter. I wanted this to be in our booth. I had it all planned, the execution of it all timed. But here you go, changing my plans," he says, and I put my hand over my mouth to stifle my excitement. It's happening. Right now. And we're going to get to hear it. I want to scream, I'm so excited.

"Then again, I guess it's fitting," he says. "Because you changed all my plans when you came here. Before you, I thought I'd never trust a woman again. I'd been burned by my mom and by so many other women, I didn't think love was worth it, you know? When you came into J & J's that first time, I was drawn to you. I could barely manage to stay focused on the tattoo because I was just overcome by… something. I didn't know what it was at the time. When I saw you again from that booth over there, I was completely taken by you. And not only because you're gorgeous. It was your energy. It was just you, Avery. Something told me you were different. I was right. For once in my life, I was completely right." Jesse's words flow into each other in a gorgeous monologue. I can tell he's nervous by how fast he's talking, but it's still beautiful. It's Jesse.

It's them.

"Jesse, what's happening?" Avery asks, her voice shaking. I think she's catching on. Uh-oh. She sounds nervous. I hope we weren't wrong in reassuring Jesse. I eye Lysander and Reed. They look nervous for Jesse, too.

"All my life, I thought love was too hard, too painful. I thought I'd focus on other things. We've both been through so much, Avery. We've both been hurt. Our hearts have been marked by regrets and lies. But when I kissed you for the first time, it all changed. You helped me see that not all marks are permanent, and some tattoos fade with time. You helped me see love was worth it."

"You helped me, too, Jesse. I love you," she says, her voice still shaky.

"And I love you, forever. You're such a permanent part of me. You've tattooed over all the past pain and doubts about love. You've given me fresh ink, so to speak, and a fresh outlook on love. I can't imagine my life without you. I don't want to. I know you've had bad experiences in the past and I know you're probably scared, but living with you these past months has shown me we can be good together for the long-haul. It's shown me we can make it, together. It won't be easy, and sometimes the past will surface. But together, we'll quiet those fears. Together, we'll build a beautiful life and walk into that horizon hand in hand. We'll jump in, all-in."

It's my cue. I know it. I shake Henry and Levi prods Jake forward.

"Hey, boys, can you come out here? Henry? Jake?"

Jesse calls.

They walk toward the swinging doors, hearing Jesse's voice. I cross my fingers that they go, that they don't ruin this moment.

"Henry, Jake, want a snack?" Jesse says now.

At the word snack, they dash toward him.

"Well, that would've been good to know," I whisper to Levi, who smiles.

Avery gasps, probably overwhelmed, as Jesse retrieves Henry and Jake.

"Look in Jake's backpack first," he says.

We hear rustling, and I smile at Reed and Lysander. Levi, now without Jake to hold on to, grabs my hand and squeezes it.

After a moment, we hear Avery gasp again. "Will you," she manages to choke out. I'm pretty sure she's crying at this point.

After another moment, we hear more rustling and Jesse must hand her the sign, because Avery says, "Are you serious?"

"I'm completely serious. I love the life we've already built together in this short amount of time, and I can't wait to see what else we could build together. I know you've been hurt before, and I know you've sworn off love. But I love you. I vow to you to be faithful and to love you forever, which isn't a word I throw around lightly. So, what do you say? Avery Johannas, will you jump in the water with me again? Will you jump all in? Will you marry me?"

I feel tears sliding down my face now, too. That man

knows what to say.

I hold my breath. *Please, Avery. Say yes.*

"When I met you, Jesse Pearce, I told myself there was a line I wouldn't cross. I wouldn't let my heart be handled by a man again. I wouldn't trust a man again with my love."

My heart sinks. Shit. This isn't good. Reed and Lysander look horrified too.

"And then, slowly, you made me want to cross that line. You made me feel safe and secure. And once I stepped over it, I realized you're different. You're this sweet and sexy man, Jesse, who makes me want to live and laugh. Most of all, you make me want to love. You make me want to explore with you. I never thought I'd be here again. I never thought I could be here again, but you've shown me anything is possible. Starting over is possible. Loving is possible. So yes, I'll jump in with you."

"Yes?" Jesse asks in disbelief.

"Yes," she says.

I jump up and down a little bit. We all give them a moment for what I imagine to be a steamy kiss.

Soon, I can't wait any longer. I let go of Levi's hand and bust through the swinging doors to the restaurant.

"Oh my God, oh my God, oh my God! Yay!" I chant like a child hopped-up on candy. I grab Avery and squeeze her so tight I think she might explode.

"I'm so happy for you!" I bubble. We're a jumping, hugging, crying mess. I pull back to admire the blue diamond on Avery's ring finger. "I told you that tattoo guy knew what he was doing," I say.

Avery laughs. "You were in on this?" she asks now, as Lysander, Reed, and Levi head out to offer congratulations to Jesse.

"Obviously we were. Do you think tattoo boy could pull off all of this without us? Please," Lysander says, and we all smile. The dogs, excited by the commotion, wander around the place now, sniffing, probably looking for a stray french fry.

"So, when is this shindig happening? Have you thought about colors yet?" Reed asks.

"Slow down, buddy. Give them a minute to breathe," Lysander says. "I think someone is just hoping to play wedding planner."

"Of course," Avery says. "We'll get back to you on the date, though."

"Yes. Right now, we've got some celebrating to do at home," Jesse says, pulling Avery in closer.

Reed lets out a wolf whistle.

"Get out of here, you crazy kids," I say, nudging Avery. "Go have wild engaged sex. See you tomorrow."

Avery winks at me as Jesse pulls her out the front door, grabbing Jake's leash as Avery grabs Henry. They stroll out the door like the happy family they are.

"I am so damn excited," I say. "We did it! It worked."

"So," Reed says, pulling me in. "What color diamond do you want, just for reference." He eyes me and then Levi strategically.

"Don't get any ideas," I say. "We're just having fun."

I look up at Levi, who smiles and winks. "Of course.

Just fun."

Reed shakes his head. "If you say so."

On the way back to the apartments, I think about the proposal and how beautiful it was. I think about what it must've felt like to be Avery, hearing those words. And although I tell myself the line in the sand Avery was talking about is clearly still in place for Levi and me, as we stroll hand in hand, I let my mind wander a little.

I start to think what it would be like to hear Levi say those magical words.

Most of all, I think about how I might actually, possibly want to say "yes."

It's just the emotion of the moment, I tell myself. Stop getting crazy ideas.

Levi and I kiss at the door to my apartment. It's a heated kiss, and I think about inviting him in.

But I don't.

The line in the sand—or in this case, the grass—needs to be protected. I've got to watch myself, or Levi Creed is going to sweep me away into dangerous, dangerous territory, whether he wants to or not.

"Good night, neighbor," I say.

"Good night," he says, but he hesitates to pull away. There's a look in his eyes that says he's thinking about that line, too—but he's thinking about crossing it.

I pull away and head inside, shutting the door. As I lean on it, exhaling, I wonder what is happening and how I'm going to make it stop.

Chapter Fourteen

"Beer, pizza, and wings. I don't know any better way to celebrate the newly engaged couple," I say, clinging to Levi's arm as we greet Avery and Jesse.

It's the Thursday night after the engagement, and we're out to celebrate at our favorite pizza place on the boardwalk. Levi and I took the bus, meeting the lovebirds for a night out. Avery is hanging on Jesse's arm. I can't help but notice her glancing at her ring as it sparkles in the light.

"Thanks for coming," Avery says to Levi, who is wearing a Lynyrd Skynyrd T-shirt and his jeans—*the* jeans—that make me all crazy inside.

"Wouldn't miss it. Congrats again," Levi says, extending a hand to Jesse, who stretches his tattooed arm. "Nice tattoos, by the way. Love the sleeve."

"Thanks. You have any?" he asks as we're led to our table by the hostess.

"No. Thought about it, but just haven't done it yet."

"Swing by some time. Jesse will take it nice and easy on you," Avery says, smiling.

"Just be careful. He has a habit of falling in love with his clients," I say as we cram into a corner booth.

"Those days are done now," Jesse says, his green eyes lighting up as he looks at Avery.

"You two are damn cute together. Honestly, whoever hooked you up deserves, I don't know, a free dinner or something."

"Well, that's part of the reason we wanted to go out tonight," Avery says as we pass around the menus—although we all know what we're getting, minus Levi.

"Oh, really? Free dinner for me?" I flash a huge smile their way.

"No, actually, we wanted to talk about what an important part of our lives you are, Jodie. In all seriousness, as much as I gave you a hard time, you were right. Jesse was it for me, and you were the one who helped me see it."

"I mean, I don't like to gloat, but…." I pause to revel in all the glory.

"I think you do," Levi says, nudging me.

"Anyway, I was hoping… well… will you be my maid of honor?"

"Are you serious?" I ask.

"Of course, silly. Who else would I pick?"

"Yes! Obviously, I will! This is so exciting. I'm going to cry," I exclaim, scooching out of the booth to run to the other side and hug her.

"Oh no, please don't start the waterworks," Jesse says.

"Better get used to it. Besides, I have my money on you bawling your eyes out at the wedding," I say to Jesse, who shakes his head.

"Tattoo-covered manly men don't cry," he says, puffing his chest out a little bit.

"Uh-huh. We'll see."

The waitress comes over and we order pizza, wings, and beer. "So, what have you two been up to these days? Anything exciting?" Avery asks me as Jesse and Levi engage in a conversation about tattoos and cars.

She winks at me lasciviously, and I know she's not asking about our mini-golf trip on Monday night or our walk on the beach.

"Nothing out of the ordinary," I say, but I can't hold the smirk back as I eye Levi. "But I've been thinking about, you know, taking things to the next level," I whisper.

"Who could blame you? I think that man gets more attractive every time I see him. What the hell are you waiting for?"

The waitress delivers the hot wings, and we pass them around. I dig in. "Well, thinking about it last night," I say through a mouthful of chicken, "I don't know. What *am* I waiting for?" I wink at Avery, who smiles and nods.

"What are you two talking about?" Jesse asks, and Levi turns his attention to me.

"Oh, just talking about the new tattoo I want to get," I lie. "Thinking about getting a quill on my shoulder. Know any skilled tattoo artists who can help me?"

"I might know a few. But I think he charges extra for

sassy clients." Jesse smiles at me and takes a swig of his beer.

"Well, then mine will be free, I guess." I smile.

"You know, if you're heading to get a tattoo, maybe I could come, too," Levi says.

"And what are you planning on getting?" I ask, intrigued. I've always liked a man with tattoos.

"I don't know. Jesse and I were just talking about my scar and possibly getting something to cover it."

I put the wing down. "You know, you don't have to do that. You're fine the way you are," I say, meaning it.

He smiles. "Thanks for saying that. It's not that I'm ashamed anymore, necessarily. I just…. I want a fresh start, you know?"

"Amen," Avery says, raising her glass.

"I'm ready to leave the past in the past. Bronc riding was an awesome part of my life, but I think it's time I let it go. Still, I'll always be grateful for the experience. I'm thinking of getting the silhouette of a bronc rider to cover the major part of the scar, just as a memento of what I used to be. It'll kind of be a way to put it to rest. I want to maybe get some Johnny Cash lyrics above it, too."

"I like it," I say. "Really. So, tattoo boy, when can we get an appointment?"

"Um, want to come by on Sunday? The shop's closed, but I could probably fit in two of my favorite people," Jesse says, grabbing another hot wing.

"Excuse me. You've known him, what, for part of the summer, and he gets favorite status? What is this?" I argue.

"He likes cars, and the rodeo thing is pretty sweet. What can I say?" Jesse smiles.

"Since you're so into him, maybe you could just move on in with him and give me Avery back. After all, I need a roommate."

"Oh, that reminds me," Jesse says, smiling. "You can't have Avery back, but I might be able to help you out. You remember Brett?"

I almost choke on the chicken wing. "How could I forget?"

"Well, long story short, he broke up with his girlfriend and needs a place to live like yesterday. I know you're looking for a roommate, so it might be a good time, you know?"

"Are you kidding?" Avery asks. "She can't live with him. That's not going to work."

"I gather you know Brett?" Levi asks, studying me.

"Um, you could say that. It was a few years ago. Never got too serious." I study the chicken wing on my plate like it's the most interesting thing ever.

"Just fun?" Levi asks, his voice uncharacteristically serious. I turn to see his eyes, which are narrowing a bit. Is it my imagination, or is his jaw clenching?

"Just a fling, you could say. Still, maybe Avery's right. Wouldn't it be weird?"

Jesse shrugs. "Just an idea. I know you need a roommate to help with rent, and it seemed like a possible solution. Besides, after the whole Gemma thing, how much worse could it get? And Brett works a ton of hours for me, so you'd have the place to yourself during the day. Could be a good option."

Levi doesn't say anything. I think about it, silently reaching for a piece of the pizza the waitress just brought over. It would be so awkward. Then again, maybe it could work out. He'd have his own room, and it can't be worse than when Gemma lived with me.

"I'll think about it, okay? I'll get back to you on Sunday."

"Okay. No pressure. Just a thought," he says. "So, Levi, tell me about the whole landlord scene. Avery told me your grandfather owns a lot of properties?"

I'm thankful for the change of subject, because things just got weirdly tense.

"I'm going to the restroom," Avery says.

"Me, too," I say.

Jesse shakes his head. "Women. Always going to the bathroom in packs. Look, I can't help it if Levi and I devour all the food while you're gone, okay?" He gives Avery a little tap on her behind, and she squeals playfully as we scamper off to the ladies' room.

Once inside, she grabs my arm. "Oh my God, Levi got jealous when Jesse brought up Brett living with you."

I eye her. "No way. You're crazy." But inside, I'm wondering if she's right. I thought I saw hints of jealousy, too, which seemed weird.

"I'm not. He got quiet and serious. This whole 'just fun' thing you two have going is a sham. Admit it. Things are much more than fun for you."

"I don't know, Avery. I think he's pretty serious about

just fun."

"And so was I," she says, giving me a look. "And now look at me." She holds up her ring.

"You know, a lesser woman would get irritated with you showing that thing off so much," I say, grinning.

"Only if she was hoping for one too," Avery replies, challenging me.

"Look, let's calm down here. I don't even know how he is in bed or anything. Stop rushing me to the altar."

"So find out," she says, matter-of-factly.

I shake my head, checking my hair and makeup before we exit the bathroom. On the way back to the table, I think maybe Avery's right. Staring at Levi's rippling biceps under his T-shirt, knowing what other hot body parts are out of sight, I shudder a little.

The kisses have been electric. The mere sight of him sends my head spinning.

Maybe it's time we take the next step and see just how much fun we could be together.

* * *

The air is muggy as we wait at the bus stop, our hands entwined. I taste pizza and beer on my breath, but it doesn't stop Levi from leaning in and stealing a kiss.

After waving goodbye to Avery and promising to talk more about plans for the big day soon, Levi and I hop on the bus.

Driving in Ocean City can be a nightmare, especially during the tourist season. Riding the bus is more convenient.

However, every time I set foot on the bus, I remember why it's worth driving or even walking.

The bus is crowded with people to the point we are lucky to find two seats in the way back. I am wedged between Levi and a man who clearly got on the bus after swimming because there are puddles and clumps of sand all around him.

Across the aisle from us, a presumably married couple argues loudly while their seven-year-old girl cries about wanting ice cream. I hear something about a mother-in-law and beach umbrellas, the woman pointing angrily at the glasses-wearing man. He looks dejected, hanging his head as she reads him the riot act. A few teenagers near the front of the bus get in trouble for break dancing in the aisle as the bus pulls out, and the man near Levi smells like he hasn't worn deodorant in a month.

It isn't quite a pleasant ride, and we've got too many streets to go.

I lean into Levi, tired from the excitement. It feels good to lean into him, to smell his oaky cologne in the midst of the scents of mildew and body odor floating around the bus.

"Are you really thinking about moving in with Brett?" he murmurs into my hair, and I pull back, looking up at him. So much for finding peace in the middle of a hellish bus.

"I don't know. I need a roommate," I confess.

"And you don't think it would be weird to live with a guy you were once close with?"

"We weren't close," I respond.

"But you had sex?" he asks pointedly.

At the word, the family across the aisle stops their argument, looking at us with exasperated faces, as if we've just committed a sin. I try to ignore them, and soon, they're back to arguing, this time about flip-flops and sandals.

"We did." There's no point in hiding it.

Levi shakes his head, exhaling loudly.

"I don't understand why this is bothering you," I say. "It was in the past. You've had plenty of women in your past, I'm sure."

"A few. But I'm not moving in with them," he says.

"It's not like that. It would be strictly financial."

"Until one day it isn't." An edge creeps into his voice. He's clearly upset.

"I don't understand why you're upset. It's not like I would do anything with Brett. Besides, we're just having fun. We've already said this isn't an exclusive, committed thing, right?" There's tension creeping into my voice, and my words are punctuated by frustration.

There is a moment's hesitation that makes me wonder if Levi is going to change his mind, is going to reveal other feelings right here on this smelly not-quite-oasis on wheels. He simply sighs.

"Look, I think it's a bad idea. I'm going to be honest with you. I don't like it. It makes me sort of... jealous."

My heart beats a little faster, and I have to tell myself to keep my smile at bay. I don't know why, but I like the thought of Levi being a little jealous.

"Okay. I just don't understand why."

He kisses my cheek, and I look up into those smoldering

dark eyes. He leans in and plants a soft kiss on my lips this time. It's sensuous and sweet at the same time, like a promise of something grand and completely worth it.

Suddenly, the dripping wet man beside me and the fighting family across from me melt away.

The body odor from a few seats over unfortunately doesn't melt away, but hey, a kiss can only be so good, right?

"Because," he whispers in my ear now, which in and of itself sends a shiver through me. I feel a chill, the kind you get when you've got a sunburn and the summer breeze goes right through you. But this isn't sunburn. This is Levi Creed, pure and simple. And sexy.

"I was liking the idea of having your place all to ourselves, of enjoying all the free space. I was entertaining all kinds of ideas of things we could do with that space, without a roommate nearby."

"But there's always your place," I reply, running a hand gently up his thigh in what I hope is pure seduction. I notice his breathing is a little ragged, so I think it's working. I try to be inconspicuous. Luckily, the husband across from me apparently pushed a button with his wife because yelling woman is now red in anger. She's not worried about the couple across from her who is getting way hot and way bothered.

"True. But the walls are paper thin, and I think there might be some noise." His eyes sparkle. He knows where he just sent my mind. I nibble on my lip, not breaking eye contact.

"Oh really, cowboy?" I whisper back after a moment.

"Mighty confident in your… skills."

Now my heart beats faster, thudding in my chest and amplifying the tension in a totally good way.

"A rodeo cowboy has to be confident."

"So, you're telling me I shouldn't have a roommate so we can enjoy… the rodeo… anytime we want? Sounds like a whole lot of fun to me."

"And maybe more," he whispers. "If I'm being honest, I've been thinking about all sorts of ways I can get that dress off you tonight."

His hand wanders up my knee, resting just underneath the hem of my dress.

My breathing is raspy, lagging.

"Come home with me tonight," I murmur, my thoughts racing with what it's going to feel like when that hand travels further up, when this dress flies across the room, when I unbutton his jeans and peel them right down.

"I've been waiting for you to say that," he says.

"Baltimore and thirty-fifth street," the bus driver mercifully announces before we've got at least fifty shades of something about to happen, public transportation and all.

"Next stop, your bed," Levi murmurs in my ear as he yanks my hand and pulls me toward the door of the bus.

***

"Your place or mine?" he asks when we get to the front lawn of the apartments.

I think about it for a moment before smiling. "Mine, this time," I say.

He tips his cowboy hat, and I unlock my door, him following closely. I don't bother with the light as he closes the door behind him. He spins me around, his hands on my waist, and before I can even think about it, he's kissing me, ferociously but sweetly, a perfect mix of rough and gentle.

I find my hands lifting his hat off his head and putting it on mine as I walk backward, leading him to my room.

"You ready for this, cowboy?" I ask in my sultriest voice as I pull back from him, his hands still on my waist.

He doesn't answer, taking the hat off my head and tossing it across the room, his brown eyes glinting in the moonlight with hunger, with lust.

I'm thrilled to be on the receiving end of that lust tonight.

The buzz from the beer isn't enough to dull my thoughts. As I back toward the bed and peel his shirt off him, my hands instantly finding his rock-hard abs, I know exactly what I'm doing. I know exactly what I'm doing when my hands slowly creep down and find the button to his jeans, Levi kicking off his cowboy boots as I slide his pants over his hips.

I know exactly what I'm doing when my hand confidently slides inside his boxers, finding him and grasping him, shuddering at the mere feel of him in my hand.

I know exactly what I'm doing when I drop to my knees and give him a real reason to lust for me, a promise he won't be changing his mind anytime soon.

I know exactly what I'm doing when I claim him as mine, when I wrangle his wild heart and rope him in with lust, and the thing is, I like it. I like being clearheaded and owning this moment willingly. True, it's fun and filled with insatiable fun, unquenchable desire. But it's more than that.

Because as I stand up and Levi rips my sundress off as promised, flinging it across my bedroom, lowering me onto the bed, slipping on a condom, and taking me in every way, my cries of pleasure are more than just sexual instinct.

They're the acknowledgment that Levi Creed is truly more than just fun or a neighbor with banging benefits sort of thing.

As I find a new height of passion, of sensuality, and of connection I've never found with anyone else, I know in that moment I'm all his, whether I want to be or not. I know I'm not going to leave this bedroom the same in any way. I know that the "just fun" mantra is true in many, many ways—but I also know that the word "just" doesn't belong between Levi Creed and me.

Because, as he rolls off me and pulls me into his arms, my head fitting perfectly on his chest, the only word I would use to describe us together in this moment is "all."

Chapter Fifteen

By Sunday, Levi and I have tried out quite a few different rooms between our apartments, and I've gotten very little sleep. We've also managed to fit in a few rounds of sex on the beach and skinny dipping in the ocean, two of my bucket list items I've crossed off a few times before—but not with a cowboy, so it's sort of a first. Last night, we also managed to fit in a skinny-dipping round in the hotel pool a few blocks down, which we snuck into after hours. This feat involved a bottle of alcohol, a dare, and climbing over a fence. Let's just say I'm showing the rodeo cowboy I can give him a run for his money when it comes to wild.

Not that either of us are complaining. The constant smile on my face certainly says I'm enjoying our new adventures, both inside and outside the bedroom. Let's just say that "just fun" has never been quite as much fun as it has been with the cowboy.

Sunday morning, though, we drag ourselves out of bed to

meet Jesse at the shop. We're still determined to go forward with the tattoos.

"You nervous?" I ask him as we head for J & J's, Jesse's tattoo shop. The other J in the name is in honor of his dad, a sweet sentiment that makes me like the place even more.

"Of course not. I'm not afraid of a little pain."

"Yeah, we'll see."

We get to the parlor, and Jesse's waiting for us. "You two didn't chicken out?"

"Of course not," I say. "Although he might."

"No way. I'm in."

"Who's going first?" Jesse asks.

"Jodie," Levi says instantly.

I turn and smile, raising an eyebrow.

"What?" he asks, shrugging it off. "Just figured yours won't take as long since it's small. That way, you can carry on with your day. You won't have to wait around."

"You think I'm going to leave and not watch you get your first tattoo? Are you kidding me? I've got to see Mr. Tough Guy in action, make sure he doesn't get the sniffles."

Jesse leads me back to the chair.

"Why? You said it doesn't hurt," Levi says. I can tell he's getting nervous even if he doesn't want to admit it.

"It doesn't. Much," I reply, grinning.

"Play nice," Jesse warns. "Dude, you'll be fine. If you could handle a rodeo, you can handle a tattoo. Nothing to it. And I guarantee once you get one, you'll be back for more. Point proven." He points to me as I pull my shirt off my shoulder to reveal the bare skin on my right one. I also pull out my phone to show Jesse the picture.

"All right, just give me some time to draw this up," he says, and I turn to see Levi chewing his nails.

I don't even think he's a nail biter.

"You know you don't have to do this," I say.

"I want to do this. I'm not the type to back down from an adventure."

"Doesn't really look like you want to do this."

"Just stop. I'm not backing out," he says.

"Suit yourself. Anyway, Jesse, where's Avery?"

"She is off to the Ocean City Lifeguard Museum. She's working on a mural there."

"That's awesome. She told me you two finally set a date," I say. She texted me last night.

"Yep. We're not rushing into anything. I want to make sure she's comfortable, you know?

"Oh, she's comfortable. Still, it's good you're giving yourselves time. Besides, June will be here before you know it."

I turn to Levi, who is being uncharacteristically quiet.

After a while, Jesse finishes the sketch and transfers the blue template onto my skin. Once I give it the go-ahead, he starts working on me with the actual tattoo machine. I can feel Levi studying me to gauge my reactions.

"Relax, cowboy, it'll be your turn soon."

"You have the picture?" Jesse asks Levi a while later, when he's finishing up on me.

Levi busies himself on his phone, pulling out the photos he found. "Right here."

Jesse puts the final touches on my tattoo, says, "All done," and leads me to the mirror.

"Love it. Not too shabby." I admire the ink in the mirror, smiling at how perfect it is. I turn to Levi. "You're up."

Levi exhales and heads to the chair to show Jesse the pic.

"Okay, want my advice?" Jesse asks.

"Sure."

"This is going to take a long time. If you're nervous, which, let's face it, you're a bit nervous, we don't have to do it all at once. Why don't we do the horse and bronc rider with the lasso for today. Then, if all goes well, you can come back for another sitting to get the background details and the lyrics finished. What do you think?"

Levi looks at me. "I don't know. I'm not the kind to go the easy way out. I kind of wanted to just go all-in."

"I get it. But it's going to be a long sitting. Let's just not go overboard, you know?"

"All right." Levi resigns himself. "But it's not because I'm afraid."

I put my hands up. "I didn't say anything of the sort." I smirk a little as Jesse gets things ready. It's obvious Levi is nervous as hell.

"Cowboy, calm down. It's going to be fine." I ease up a little, taking pity on him.

And twenty minutes later, when Jesse starts the tattoo, Levi exhales loudly. "Shit, this isn't half as bad as I thought."

"Told you. What, you don't trust me?" I roll my eyes from my corner seat.

"I wouldn't trust you, either. I mean, look what you did to

poor, defenseless Gemma. She's probably having to hustle on the boardwalk now and living above the boardwalk french fry shop." Jesse says, eying me with a smirk.

I scowl. "Do *not* bring up Gemma. I'm sure she's just fine. Probably already has a house and a ring from a new Home Depot guy."

"God bless him, if so," Jesse says. "Anyway, did you think on the roommate thing?"

"I did." I'm glad Levi is on his stomach and not looking at me.

"And?" Jesse asks.

"I don't know. I kind of think it would be awkward with Brett. Nothing personal."

Jesse stops the gun for a minute, raising an eyebrow. "Of course. Nothing personal." He shakes his head in judgment. "But I get it. It's just, now you'll have to find a roommate, and soon. Wonder where you could ever find someone who would want to live with you."

I get exactly what he's suggesting, and my face burns. "I don't know. I'm sure I'll think of something." I could kill Jesse right now. As I said, the only saving grace is I can't see Levi's face or eyes.

"I'm sure you will," Jesse says.

***

"I'm so excited. It looks good, doesn't it? So awesome," Levi observes as we head back to the apartment complex after several hours. I get it, though. That first tattoo is a rush.

"I think it looks pretty damn good. Are you going to

seriously get the background done?"

"Yeah, of course. And maybe I'll get some kind of half-sleeve or something too."

"Easy, cowboy. Let's not get crazy here."

He takes my hand in his and swings our arms, clearly in a good mood. Must be all the extra adrenaline from the tattoo.

"Hey, question. Do you work tomorrow night?" he asks.

"Um, no. I work the morning shift tomorrow."

"You think you want to go to a barbecue? Apparently, Jesse was telling me there's this place called Fager's Island?"

"Oh, yeah. They've got these amazing Monday night deck parties. Love the food."

"Want to go? Figured it might be good to get out and do some sightseeing, check out more of the local haunts."

"And barbecue is right up your alley, huh?"

"You bet."

"Perfect. I'll see if Avery and Jesse want to go?" I ask.

"Or, you know, we could go just us," he slips in.

Like a date.

It's not like I'm shocked. We've been out plenty of times now alone. But that was before we crossed the sex bridge.

"Sounds like a fun time," I say, emphasis on the fun. I just feel like we're in murky waters now, like the line is going to get blurred.

"I thought so. Perfect. Oh, and Jodie?"

"Yeah?"

"I'm glad you said no to Brett. Now, don't get all crazy

and think I'm trying to box this in or take things to a more serious level. I'm just glad, is all."

"Me too. I think it would've been weird. I'm just worried about rent and all. I mean, I can get by for a few more months."

"I'm sure it'll work out," he says, squeezing my hand as we head back to the apartments and go our separate ways, both needing to get some work done before night falls and we are otherwise preoccupied.

"Your place or mine tonight?" he asks, and I smile, shaking my head.

"I mean, maybe we should just take tonight off. I'm sure your back is going to hurt and all from the tattoo."

"No worries. I'm tough. I can suck it up for the right reasons," he says, and I smile.

"This is starting to sound like some bad romantic comedy," I observe. "But how about my place? I don't think we've, um, checked out the laundry room yet?"

"I like how you think," he says, and he kisses me feverishly before giving my ass a slap and heading to his apartment, Johnny Cash squawking at his return.

***

I wear the new red sundress Avery helped me pick out when we went shopping last week. It hugs me in all the right places, and I feel good in it. I spend some extra time doing my makeup, watching some YouTube tutorials to get it just right—not Gemma's, just to be clear. I shave my legs, fluff my hair, and put on the jewelry I reserve for special occasions.

It feels over the top for a deck party on a Monday, but I guess that's the thing about the sexy cowboy. He makes me feel sexier. He makes me want to look sexy. He makes me want to look as good as he makes me feel.

He picks me up at 4:00 p.m., and we head to the bus stop, hand in hand as we are so often these days. We ride the bus so neither of us has to drive through the crazy traffic. We chat about our workdays until we reach Fager's Island.

Inside, we buy tickets for the famous Monday night barbecue and wait in line.

"I can't believe how cheap this is," Levi says. "It feels like we're stealing."

"It kind of does. Best ribs you'll ever have."

"I don't know. You haven't tried mine yet. But we'll see."

The line is winding through the deck area of the restaurant, the ribs sizzling on the grill. They smell heavenly.

We look out to the bay, the water lapping on the sand near the bar. "It's beautiful here," Levi says.

I nod in agreement. "It is. Sometimes I forget how lucky we are to live in such a pretty place. Do you miss Texas, though?" I ask now, seeing a wistfulness in his eyes.

He shrugs. "A little, yeah. It's just different here. I miss the rodeo and my friends. I miss my parents sometimes. It's just different."

"Different in a good way, though?"

"Mostly, yeah. When I left home for here, I didn't know if I'd be happy. I figured I'd just come for the summer and see, you know? When my grandfather made the offer,

I thought it seemed reasonable, but I honestly didn't see myself making a life here. Some small-town, music-loving country boy living the beachy, tourist attraction life? Didn't seem right."

"And now?" I ask, a little bit afraid to hear the answer, afraid to admit how devastated I'll be if he says what I don't want to hear. Waiting for Levi to tell me if he's planning to stay, if he's happy here, is terrifying.

And it is in that terror that I realize this "just fun" situation is going to fall to pieces any second. If he's planning on the long-term here, eventually we're going to have to reexamine this plan to avoid a committed relationship.

"Now," he says, and my heart beats faster, "I'm happy. Happier than I ever thought I could be. Sure, this isn't quite the job I saw myself doing. But it's not about the job. I've found a place to call home, a place where I fit. I found a place I like to explore and see. Most of all, I found someone to do that with." He leans down and kisses me, right in the middle of the line, and I feel my heel pop. He dips me a bit, and the kiss gets passionate. We even get a catcall from a drunk at the bar.

He pulls back, grinning. "Sorry. Couldn't help myself. Damn, this dress looks good."

I stare up at him with a mixture of lust and… what? I'm not sure.

All I know is Levi is a hell of a lot of fun, but it's not just that. When I'm with him, when I'm on his arm, I'm happy, too. Happier than I ever thought I could be.

The line finally moves, and we get our ribs, corn on the

cob, coleslaw, and baked beans. We squeeze into a tiny table, and Levi gets us a round of drinks.

Twenty minutes later, we're both up to our elbows in barbecue sauce and talking about how good the dinner is.

"Okay, I'll admit. I know my way around making a good rib sauce. But this is the best damn rib sauce I've ever had."

"Told you," I say.

"Yeah. I think I could definitely be happy here for good," he says after he's finished his ribs and is working on some of mine I can't eat.

"Because they have good ribs?" I ask, teasing.

He eyes me from across the table, holding up a rib. "I mean, yeah, mostly because of that. But a little bit because of the girl I'm eating ribs with."

It might be because it's August and sweltering hot, or it might be because I've just eaten too many ribs, but I feel a fluttering in my chest. I feel like I might melt right there sitting across from Levi Creed.

I feel like I'm getting in way, way too deep to turn around now.

Chapter Sixteen

This is what it feels like when everything falls apart. This is what it feels like when your dreams and goals are a disastrous wash of the word "no."

Tears stream down my cheeks as I mope on my couch, playing *Teen Mom* but not really paying attention. I see the familiar faces, but I don't connect. Everything's lost.

I spend the day like this, ignoring texts other than to lie to Avery that I'm okay after she sends me about ten messages.

Avery: Are you sure.

Me: Yeah. Just tired and feel like I'm coming down with something. Shopping this weekend, right? See you Saturday morning if not before.

I've spent the day wallowing on the sofa, Sebastian at my side. I've only gotten up to pee and to eat a few crackers.

A knocking on my door around 6:00 p.m. startles me. I mute the television to try to pretend I'm not here. I just can't face anyone right now.

"Jodie, I know you're in there. Paper-thin walls, remember?" he says. I sit silently, hugging my knees to my chest.

"Jodie? Come on. Don't make me kick down the door because then my grandfather will have to charge you for it. Come on."

I sigh, knowing he's right. I can't avoid everyone forever. Might as well own up to my loser status.

I trudge to the door in my pajama pants and T-shirt, flinging it back like I've done so many times.

"Hey, just wanted to see if you wanted to come over for dinner."

"Not hungry," I murmur.

"What's wrong?" he asks, looking startled. "And don't tell me nothing. I've heard you listening to *Teen Mom*."

"So?"

"So. I can tell something's up. Just spill."

I usher him in, and he takes a seat on the sofa next to Sebastian, who is still sleeping. "I turned in my manuscript with the changes I needed to make."

"And?" Levi asks. "Isn't that a good thing?"

"It should be. Except the editor hates what I've done. Said the book is going in a completely unmarketable direction and just isn't good. He said my Jodie spark is missing. I'm done. We're behind schedule already, and now this will delay release." Tears stream now.

Levi pulls me into him, hugging me. "Hey, it can't all be bad. Do you get to redo them?"

"Yeah, but that's the problem. I thought *this* was good. I

have no idea where to start."

"Then give yourself a break. Take some time to mull it over."

"I don't have a ton of time. I only have a few weeks, and I'm stumped," I say, tears still streaming. "It's hopeless. I'm not a good writer. This dream is a joke."

"Stop. I will not sit here while you throw a pity party and put yourself down. Dammit, do you want to be an author?"

"Obviously," I reply through my tears.

"Then do it. The Jodie I know doesn't back down from a challenge. Hell, the Jodie I know stomped over to my apartment three days after I got here to tell me to shut the parrot the hell up, all while wearing scandalously thin margarita pajamas."

I sniffle. "I was hoping you didn't notice how thin they were."

"Oh, I noticed. Trust me, I noticed. But that's not the point. You're this fearless, go-get-it woman. The editor didn't like what you did? So what. Try again. You've got this."

I sigh. "Maybe you're right."

"Maybe?" he asks, like I've just said the most ridiculous thing ever.

"Okay, you're right. I just need to take a few days to regroup and then get back to it. I'm sure I can figure it out."

"That's my girl. Now, while you're sorting through, why don't you come have dinner with me? Take the night off. Get out of this apartment. A night with me, and all your creative juices will be sparked, guaranteed or your money back."

I raise an eyebrow. "You know, I think this creative juice problem might be your fault, come to think of it. This whole writing problem only started when you moved in."

"That's because you just have such a gorgeous muse next door, the horror genre doesn't fit. Maybe you should switch to steamy romance," Levi says, smirking.

"Come on. You're so smug."

"And you're amazing. Now let's go. Go change out of your pajamas. Or don't. But meet me at my place in twenty minutes. Be prepared to be wowed. I've been cooking up a storm all day."

I sigh, smiling at him as I wipe at my eyes. "How do you do that?"

"What?" he asks.

"Make me feel like everything's going to be fine."

"Just my Texan charm, I guess," he says. "Seriously. Stop stressing out. You've got this. I believe in you."

As he stands from the couch and heads out the door, things don't seem so bad. Just the fact that he believes in me might be enough to get me through.

***

"Smells amazing," I say when I stroll into his apartment wearing my jean shorts and a T-shirt. I figured there was no need to go all out. He already saw me in pajamas and crying today.

Johnny Cash squawks at me, and I walk over to the cage to say hello. He starts whistling a little piece of a song I taught him last week, and I clap my hands in excitement.

"Did you hear that?" I ask Levi as he strolls over to me.

"See. Told you that you were wrong about him."

"Okay, he's still annoying. But I'll admit, that's pretty neat."

Levi pulls me to the little table in his kitchen. It's set with actual plates, silverware, and even a little votive candle in the middle.

"Wow, you went all out," I say.

"As much as a bachelor can, I suppose. Not exactly fine linens, but it'll do, right?" He pulls out my chair for me, and I sit down.

"Have you seriously been cooking all day?" I ask as he pulls out a pan from the oven.

"You think I'm going to let an Ocean City barbecue show up a Texan? Come on. I was born making barbecue," he says, grinning. "And yes, I've been cooking all day."

"What if I'd been busy tonight?" I ask.

"Then I'd have changed your mind." He winks at me.

"And what if it hadn't worked?"

"In the highly unlikely chance it didn't, I'd have had a lot of barbecue to myself, then."

He brings over a rack of ribs for my plate and then his, precariously carrying them in metal tongs across the kitchen. My plate looks like a caveman's, but smells amazing. Levi also brings over a bowl of chili for each of us, and a pan of cornbread.

"Now this is some true Texan eating," he says. "Mama's recipes and all."

I smile. "Thank you for this."

"You're welcome," he says seriously now. "It's nice to have someone to share a piece of home with."

I dig in, and in truth, they are the best damn ribs I've ever had. "These are so good," I say, covered in barbecue sauce. It's not the most graceful meal I've eaten on a date, but it doesn't matter. That's the thing. With Levi, even though I joke about him judging me, I know he never is. He's got this confidence in himself that never crosses the line into arrogance or condescension. He just knows who he is, and he appreciates everyone else for who they are.

He's this perfect concoction of sexy, confident, and down-to-earth. I don't know how he pulls it off.

"Why are you smiling at me?" he asks. "Not that I'm complaining."

"Just, you."

"Okay, I'll take it, I guess?"

I put down my rib and wipe my face before looking at him. "It's just, you're perfect. Seriously. Every guy I meet who is super sexy and super charming turns out to be an ass. I don't get that vibe from you. I mean, sure we joke about you being smug and all that, but, I've never felt more accepted with anyone. Like, there is no other man I could go on a date with and coat myself in barbecue sauce and not think twice."

He smiles. "That right there sounds like a perfect country song."

"Shut up. Maybe I take it all back."

"I hope not," he says, his brown eyes studying mine. "Because I think you're pretty great, too. Every attractive, charming woman I've met has, likewise, turned out to be not such a great person. I don't get that vibe from you either."

"Well, look at us, two amazing catches that no one has snatched up," I joke, reaching for my beer.

"I guess we'll just have to be thankful for that. Their loss, right, and our gain."

After dinner, I offer to help with the dishes, but Levi bats me away. "Get out of here. That's so boring. Let's have some fun."

"What do you have in mind?" I ask, winking.

"That fun can wait. Come on," he says, pulling me outside.

In the front yard, we head to his trusty fire pit. Levi leads me to a folding chair near the pit, gets a fire roaring, and hands me a stick propped against the ring. He also hands me a marshmallow.

"I haven't roasted marshmallows in forever. I'm so excited," I say, meaning it.

Levi also grabs a marshmallow and a stick, and we get to toasting.

"Back home, I'd do this all the time with my friends. We used to have fires almost every weekend."

"Did you sing campfire songs?" I ask, grinning.

"Okay, that's it. At some point, you're going to have to come to Texas with me because something tells me you have this stereotypical view of us Texans."

"But are my views wrong? Did you sing campfire songs?" I ask, prodding further as I pull my marshmallow out of the flame.

Levi grins. "Okay, sometimes we'd sing songs. But that doesn't mean you're right about everything else."

"Well, I think it's charming. I would love to see Texas sometime. I'd love to hear all the stories about the wild, untamable Levi Creed, and get the truth about this horse stealing story you refuse to give me the details about."

He grins. "Well, sometime we'll go, then. If you think my cooking is awesome, wait until you try my mom's."

The fire casting a glow on us, I get lost in the sights and sounds of the summer night with Levi. I think about how crazy fun it would be to go to Texas. Despite my adventurous, try-anything-once mantra, I haven't been able to travel that much. It would be awesome to change that, and it would be great to do it with Levi.

When we finish our marshmallows, Levi heads inside to get his phone and a speaker. He sets it up and puts on some music before reaching for my hand. He tugs me out of my chair as the music softly plays, and pulls me into him beside the fire.

"Dance with me?" he asks, and I grin wildly. Of course Levi Creed would ask me to dance on the front lawn by his probably illegal fire pit at our apartment. I oblige, though, putting my hands on his shoulders as he wraps his hands around my waist. As we sway, I look up into his brown eyes, listening closely to the song choice.

"Is this…?" I ask, as he takes the beer out of my hand and puts it in the yard. The sky is clear, and I notice how perfect the stars look as he pulls me closer.

"Johnny Cash's 'Folsom Prison Blues.' First song that

was playing when you saw me naked." He smirks. "Closest thing to a first song I could think of."

I roll my eyes and smile as I lean into him, swaying in the front yard, and not caring if anyone is watching. This isn't quite the romantic song you'd imagine slow dancing to, but it's all good in this moment. In Levi's arms, it fits. It just fits.

His arms wrapped around my waist, I nuzzle into his neck, realizing I'm feeling at peace. Despite all the chaos in my life, the roommate situation, and everything else, I don't feel anything but happy right now. He does that to me. He makes me want to be adventurous and have fun, but he also makes me want to settle into him. He makes me want to just take a step back and breathe.

I look up into his eyes, and he pushes a strand of hair out of my face. "Tonight's been amazing. Thank you for breaking me out of my craziness," I say. "I needed that."

"What are neighbors for?" he whispers before taking my lips with his.

The kiss is sweet and soft, and he takes his time. It's not the wild, passionate kisses we usually enjoy together. This kiss is different.

And when he leads me into his apartment later, kicking the door shut with his boot, it feels different, too. There's not the lusty rush to get undressed or the fiery passion that leads to ravenous, clawing hands pulling at clothes.

It's slow this time, as if we're drinking each other in. Levi picks me up once we're in the door and carries me to his bedroom, where he gently puts me down on the comforter.

He stares at me for a long moment, and it looks like he's going to say something.

I guess he changes his mind, because the next thing I know, he's beside me on the bed, kissing me gently, his hand in my hair pulling my face closer.

"You're beautiful," he whispers again. "And you're amazing. Never doubt that."

And looking into his eyes in his bedroom, I believe it. I believe that I'm beautiful and amazing and all those other things I have so much trouble seeing. Behind the wild Jodie cloak, I realize I'm vulnerable. With Levi, though, I'm okay with showing that vulnerability because I know he'll protect me.

We make love, but I know it's different this time. It's still wildly fun and wildly intoxicating, but it's something more too.

It's this knowledge of safety and security in his arms. It's the feeling of understanding not only Levi, but how he sees me, how he sees the world.

It's this unveiling of who I really want to be, and how I feel like that woman with him.

And most of all, as I fall asleep in his arms, it's the realization that thinking about this lasting forever might not be as scary as I once thought.

Chapter Seventeen

By Saturday, the book situation is no longer my biggest dilemma.

My heart is.

When Avery picks me up for our shopping adventure, I climb into her car with cups of coffee for both of us and enough confusion to fill the trunk.

"Hey. What's going on with you?" Avery asks as I hop in, my sunglasses a shield not strong enough to feign that I'm fine.

I sigh as Avery heads toward the Tanger Outlets. "Everything."

"Well, traffic's a little rough this morning, so we have plenty of time to chat about it. Spill."

So I fill Avery in on the book situation.

"Hey, you've got this, right?" she asks.

"Yeah, I guess. I've mulled it over and figured out where things went wrong."

Avery turns to me when we get to the stoplight. "The book isn't the biggest issue."

I shake my head. "I feel like you're my mom."

"Watch it, I'm not that much older than you."

"I just mean you always know when something's wrong."

"Living with a person will do that," Avery says. "Now come on. Tell me the rest."

"The book thing was bothering me. And then something happened with Levi." I sip on my coffee, putting off having to put it all into words. For being a writer, I'm terrible at explaining how I feel.

"Wait, I thought you already slept together? I'm confused now."

"We did. But, well, we slept together last night… and it was different. We were different." I glance out the window, noticing a convertible of bikini-clad girls singing and dancing wildly to their bumping music—and despite their obvious confidence, they're not really that good dancers. It looks like fun, though, and I smile, despite the situation.

Avery smirks. "You're falling in love with him. You're falling in love with each other."

I turn my attention back to our conversation. "I mean, no. Yes. I don't know. It's just so damn confusing. We both kind of promised to keep it light and fun. I don't want to get all invested in something that won't work out. But this whole keeping it fun thing is becoming work."

"Did you tell Levi how you feel?"

"Of course not."

"Why the hell not? Last year, you sure pushed me enough

to tell Jesse how I felt. Hypocrite."

I bury my face in my hands.

"I know. It's just… damn, it's not that simple. Levi's this wild child. Like we've talked so many times about how he's not interested in a relationship anymore, and neither am I. We've both been very, very clear that this is just a fun time."

"But sometimes things change, you know? Maybe you planned on it being fun, but now that's not working. I've seen the way you two are together. I know it's so much more than what you're letting on. And I know that goes both ways."

"I just don't want to ruin anything."

"Well, I think pretending it's lighter than it is might ruin something, you know?" She looks at me pointedly, and I sigh.

"I don't know. But enough about me. How's it feel being engaged?" We are pulling up to the outlet parking lot, and Avery parks by our starting point. We've done this quite a few times, and we've got our shopping route mapped.

Avery smiles. "It's great. I mean, nothing's physically changed. But it just feels… different. A good different. I never thought I'd be thinking about saying 'I do' again, but with Jesse, it doesn't feel the same. It's like, I don't know, I'm where I'm meant to be."

"So sappy," I say, rolling my eyes as we get out of the car. "But adorable. I'm happy for you. Did you talk to your parents?"

Now Avery is rolling her eyes. "Unfortunately."

"Uh-oh. I thought by now they'd warm up to the idea of

you and Jesse." Things had been rough going since Avery moved in with him. Avery's parents are a bit… different than Jesse. And they don't quite see the attraction. Her mom is also a little upset about the whole Avery blowing off the family business situation.

"Not even close. Mom seems to be in mourning, and Dad's in denial. He tries to be supportive, but I think he's under the impression this phase will wear off. But I'm at a stage of my life that I'm not going to worry about it. This is what I want. I need to focus on that. I don't even know if they're going to come for the wedding at this point."

"Are you kidding? I'm sure they'll come. You're their daughter, and even if they don't fully approve, they have to see you're happy."

"You'd think," Avery says, holding open the door to the first store as a gush of air slaps into my face. It feels heavenly, the day stifling and muggy again. "I'm not too worried, though. Jesse and I have talked, and we want to keep the wedding super simple. I thought maybe since it's his first wedding, he'd want the whole big shindig."

I laugh. "Are you kidding? I'm pretty sure Jesse would be on a plane to Vegas if he could."

"I didn't want to rip him off, though, you know? I've done the whole wedding thing, but he hasn't. Plus, I don't know, it kind of feels like a first wedding for me. Now that I see what love can really be like. I know, cue sappiness alert again. But I don't want to just have something too simple and act like this doesn't matter."

"I get it. Plus, I would kill you if you eloped. Don't

you dare steal my maid of honor duty." I smile. "I need the chance to wear a hideous dress, after all."

"You really think I'm going to put you in a hideous dress? You jerk. You have no faith. Plus, our trusty wedding planner wouldn't hear of it. You better believe everyone is going to be on point."

"If you and Jesse want simple, I'm not sure putting Reed in any position of power was a good idea."

"You're telling me. He's already called me five times about flowers, and we're not getting married until June. I think Reed's more of a bridezilla in this wedding than me."

I smile as we paw through some racks of clearance clothes, pulling out options and giving feedback.

"It's crazy how much has changed since last summer, huh?" I say nonchalantly as I pull out a red sundress, thinking about how much Levi liked me in the other red dress.

"It is. Life changes so fast. Who knows what will be happening next year? Maybe there will be two weddings," Avery says, smirking and winking at me.

"Well, don't look at me. I can't even agree to boyfriend/ girlfriend status with my guy."

Avery smiles bigger.

"What?" I ask.

"You called him your guy. Same thing. I knew that cowboy was going to be good for you."

I roll my eyes, and we continue shopping, traveling down the outlet strip to all our favorite stores, buying way too much, and giggling about everything from Gemma to

Avery's mother's horror at the wedding. It feels good to be with her, like old times, escaping from our dramas and questions back home.

"Avery?" I say as we're sitting at our favorite pizza shop for lunch, waiting for food.

"Yeah, Jo?"

"I'm so glad you moved here. Seriously. Best thing that ever happened to my boring life."

"Well, one of the top two at least. I know someone else who moved here who has been pretty great in your life, too."

I groan. "Can't you see I'm trying to have a sentimental moment? Do you always have to bring it back to the Texan?"

"Listen, all I have to say is I'm glad I moved here too. So you and that cowboy better not get any crazy ideas to go off back to Texas, do you hear me?"

"Never," I say, smiling and meaning it. "This is home. This is where my family is."

"Me too," Avery replies, looking a little teary-eyed. "Now dammit, stop being so sentimental. I want to eat my pizza without crying like a psycho."

"Hey, I'm just building up your tolerance for the wedding. Because once you hear my maid of honor speech, you're going to bawl like a baby."

"I guarantee it," she says, shaking her head. "Love you."

"Love you, too," I say, thinking about how true it is.

Chapter Eighteen

August shutdown comes around—Lysander's words for the monthly Midsummer Night's shutdown in order to party. I couldn't be more thankful.

To be clear, the last thing I should be doing is heading to the club and buying expensive drinks. Money's getting tighter without Gemma's half of the rent, and there are no book royalties in sight at this point, especially with the editing holdup. I'm getting desperate.

Not that I'm admitting it. Avery, Lysander, and even Levi would be shelling out cash to me in a second if they thought I was in such a dire situation, but I don't want that. Jodie doesn't take handouts.

Well, unless they're in the form of free drinks. Then I lower my principles a notch. I'm not foolish, after all.

But it is getting nerve-wracking, even for me. I did the unthinkable yesterday—I scanned Craigslist. I know, I'm a glutton for punishment. I even managed to convince myself

Gemma was the exception, and the next roommate would probably be amazing.

Tonight, though, I'm not worrying about it. Tonight, I'm going to go out and drink—the cheapest drinks on the menu. I'm going to dance and have fun. Just fun.

Which is good, because Levi's coming along thanks to Lysander's insistence that we take the cowboy out and show him what partying really looks like.

I'm wearing the new red dress I bought with Avery at the outlets, an off-the-shoulder number that shows off my newest tattoo. I've perfected my lips and makeup, and am feeling pretty good in my platform wedges.

My door flies open a few minutes before 7:00 p.m. "We're here. Where the hell is everyone?" Reed asks, noticing it's just me. My apartment was chosen as the meeting locale tonight because Reed and Lysander apparently have something "exciting" planned.

"On their way, I'm sure. Now, what's this text you sent about an exciting change of plans?" I ask, a little nervous.

Reed smiles. "Well, the club is great, don't get me wrong. But we're falling into a rut. Plus, with the sexy cowboy being semi-new in town, I thought it was time we show him a different side of Ocean City."

"What does that mean?" I ask, seriously worried.

"We're going to the pier and the doing the whole touristy thing!"

Reed smiles, but I just stare, cocking my head. "The pier? You mean, like, the crazy rides and carnival games part of the boardwalk? The little souvenir shops and people in costumes looking to make a buck? That's what we're doing tonight?"

"Don't be so boring. Come on. You love the carnival and funnel cake," Lysander says.

"Oh, I do. Don't get me wrong, I do. It just seems so… family-friendly for you two."

"Don't stress. There's a lovely boardwalk bar at the end we can visit. I just thought it would be fun to make new memories," Reed says.

"And you went with this?" I ask Lysander.

He shrugs. "I don't get in his way when he comes up with a plan."

My door swings open again, this time for Jesse and Avery. Behind them, Levi trudges in, smiling. Tonight, he's wearing jeans and his boots, but a royal blue muscle shirt that shows off… well, his rippling muscles. He's ditched the hat, his dark hair styled but not too styled.

He looks amazing, his tan skin popping against the royal blue.

"Look what we found. A not-so-cowboy cowboy on the front lawn."

"You look assimilated. I mean, the cowboy hat looks good, but this works for you. Beachy with a Southern edge. Yes," Reed says, giving him the stamp of approval.

"Figured the cowboy hat might be a little much in the club," Levi says, walking across the room to give me a kiss and then pet Sebastian, who is snoring on the couch despite all the company.

"Well, apparently there is no club in your future. Reed has other plans," I say, smiling.

"What are we doing now?" Jesse asks, having been around enough to know that if Reed oversees the plans, it could be frightening.

"We're going to the boardwalk, the pier area. I thought we could visit the carnival, grab some drinks at the end of the boardwalk, do the whole tourist thing in honor of our newest non-tourist in the group."

Jesse shrugs. "I rock at the carnival games. We could win some new toys for Jake and Henry."

"I want funnel cake! And to ride the Ferris wheel," Avery says, jumping up and down.

"Sounds fun to me," Levi says. "Haven't spent much time on the boardwalk."

"Well, guess we're bringing out the inner children in us, tonight. Let me get better walking shoes, and let's go," I say, grinning.

It's a different kind of shutdown night, but it could be fun. Knowing this crew, it will be a little bit crazy and not quite family friendly.

I change into my ballet flats that are super comfortable, grab Levi's arm, and head for the bus station.

***

"You're on," Levi says, shaking hands with Jesse as they walk to the dart-throwing game, deciding to put their masculinity at stake at some carnival games.

Avery and I stand back, eating cotton candy and funnel cake. "So much for watching my calories tonight," she says.

"You've got plenty of time to worry about the wedding

dress fitting. Besides, we burned some calories walking out onto the pier."

"This is really fun, you know?" Avery says as she cheers for Jesse at the game.

"It is. Where are Lysander and Reed?" I ask, turning around.

"They went into the souvenir shop around the corner."

"Oh no. Who knows what they'll buy."

Levi raises his arms in a cheer, Jesse shaking his head. Apparently Levi was victorious in their man-child face-off at the carnival game. There are actually some children in line waiting patiently behind them. I shake my head as Levi marches over, handing me a stuffed walrus.

"My lady," he says, bowing a little as he presents the cheaply made toy.

"Why, thank you," I say, passing him some remnants of my cotton candy in exchange.

"Sorry, babe. The damn cowboy is apparently a pro at rodeo and carny games," Jesse says, sulking a bit.

Avery kisses him before stuffing a piece of funnel cake in his mouth. "No worries. You'll get him next time."

"We should hit the rides next," Jesse says. "I could go for some time with you on the Ferris wheel."

"Oh, no. I sense some rocking of the cart is going to be happening," I say, winking. Jesse winks back, and we all laugh.

"Hey, guys!" Reed and Lysander shout, running out of the souvenir shop with bags and bags of items. "You should have come with us. They had some cool stuff."

"Wait a second," I say, eying Reed. "You have a souvenir shop of your own. Why are you buying stuff here?"

"I'd like to think of it as supporting other businesses."

I shake my head as the two walk proudly over to show us their treasures.

"We got some cool T-shirts for ourselves," Lysander says. "And we bought a few presents for you guys."

Reed digs in his bag, handing me a coffee mug that is X-rated, showing off a lot of male anatomy. "Oh my God, what is this?" I shriek, embarrassed and trying to hide the mug before the families around us see it.

"I mean, Jodie, do I really have to explain it to you? Thought it would keep you company in that lonely apartment when the neighbor's busy," he says, winking.

I toss it back in the bag.

"So unappreciative," he says, laughing. "Oh, and I've got something for said neighbor."

Levi widens his eyes. "After that, I'm not sure if I want it," he says, smiling.

Reed hands him a box of saltwater taffy. "I mean, it's just a given you have to have a box of this not-so-great taffy. Figured I'd buy you one to commemorate your touristy night."

Levi pretends to wipe his brow. "Thank you," he says, opening the box to eat a taffy.

"Oh, and we've got something for the adorable soon-to-be-married couple," Lysander says, plucking something out of his bag.

"How the hell did you do so much shopping in like ten minutes?" I ask.

"We're pros. Here you go," they say, handing Avery and Jesse an Ocean City spoon rest. "Seemed like a wedding-like thing to buy."

"Thanks," Avery says, smiling.

"Hold up. Why am I the only one who got a raunchy gift?" I ask.

"First, you have no idea what items we bought each other. They're in the bottom of the bag," Lysander says, grinning. "And second, because you're the serially single one of the group, by choice. I mean, if that were to change," he says, eying Levi, "maybe you'd get more normal gifts."

"I doubt it. But thank you. I will drink from my mug with pride."

"Okay, can we move on from phallic mugs? I want to hit the Ferris wheel," Avery says, mercifully changing the subject.

"Sounds fun," Reed says.

Levi hangs back a bit. "I have something else in mind for you and me," he whispers to me.

"Oh yeah?"

He pulls me to the side and points to the roller coaster.

The one that goes upside down.

"What do you say? I think two wild ones need some more excitement than a Ferris wheel."

My stomach knots just looking at what I can only view as a metal contraption of death.

"Let's stick with the group," I respond, trying to brush it off.

Levi raises an eyebrow. "Hold up. Don't tell me the

fearless Jodie Ellison is afraid of roller coasters."

"I'm not afraid," I say, faking confidence. "I just… it doesn't look safe. Not that one."

"You're afraid. Admit it," he teases.

I sigh as we follow the group to the rides portion of the boardwalk. "Okay, maybe a little. I've never liked roller coasters."

"But you've never had someone like me to hold you tight," he says, matter-of-factly.

I shake my head. "I don't know. What if I puke up cotton candy on you?'

"I'll charge you for the shirt."

"Let me guess, you'll tack it onto my rent," I reply.

"Nope. I can think of other, way more fun ways for you to make up for it," he says, winking.

I roll my eyes. "I'm going to puke now," I tease.

"I doubt it. But come on. Seriously. Live a little."

I bite my lip. The roller coaster is damn high and seriously doesn't look trustworthy.

But if this is how I die, strapped to Levi's arm, plummeting to my death after delicious cotton candy, I guess it's worth the risk.

"Hey, guys," I yell to the group. "Levi and I are going to go on the roller coaster instead."

The four of them eye the roller coaster I'm now pointing at.

"Of course you are." Avery smiles. "Of course the Ferris wheel would be too normal for you two. Reckless. I like it."

"Nice knowing you," Lysander teases as they head to

their calm, romantic moment… and Levi and I head to what I hope is just a bunch of screaming, and not our deaths.

***

"Admit it, it was awesome," Levi says, smiling ear to ear when we get off the roller coaster.

We, obviously, survived. But I screamed a whole lot of expletives on the way down. I turn to Levi. "You know what, it actually was. Such a rush. I'm glad we did it."

"And look, we have this lovely commemorative picture to remember it," he says, teasing me as he points to the picture we bought at the booth after the ride was over. It's one of those cameras that snaps your picture when you're coming off the biggest dip. Levi is giving a thumbs-up and smiling at the camera.

I am greenish and leaning into Levi's arm, my head buried.

"We are not putting that up," I say.

"I have the perfect place right inside the entranceway," he says, and I punch his arm.

"You're terrible."

"You love it," he says.

As we regroup with Lysander, Reed, Avery, and Jesse, I squeeze his hand. "Yeah, I guess I kind of do."

"So now where to?" Reed asks, the four of them looking blissfully at peace, while Levi and I are a ball of energy from our experience.

"Oh, I've got the perfect idea for how to finish out our touristy night," I say. "Follow me."

The group shrugs, following me down the boardwalk to make one last memory.

***

"Why does he get to be the cowboy?" Lysander whines, dressed as a gangster along with Reed and Jesse.

Avery and I are in very short flapper outfits. I'm trying not to think about how many bodies have been in this thing, but still. It smells a little funky.

"Because it just made sense," I say, smiling at Levi who is the only one of us who looks comfortable.

"It doesn't make sense for a cowboy in a picture of gangsters and flappers," Lysander argues.

"Can we just take this picture and act like you're having fun?" I complain.

The photographer looks annoyed, as we've already changed costumes a few times and argued about positioning in the photograph. We've taken up way too much of his time.

He takes a photo, and then says, "Okay, now a silly one." He's an older gentleman who hasn't smiled a single smile since we've gotten here, and now looks like he's already regretting those words.

Reed and Lysander jump on the mock bar setup. I have visions of it breaking. Jesse sidles up to Avery, and they do a *Charlie's Angels* pose.

Levi grabs me and dips me, kissing me hard.

I come up from the kiss after the photo has been taken, desperately needing air.

"Oh yeah, that's my favorite one. We're definitely

getting a print of it," Levi announces.

Reed sneaks up to peek at the preview. "Oh, look how many adorable, quirky photos you two will have for your home when you finally admit how you feel."

And then he scampers away to change back into his clothes, complaining about the itchy collar of his shirt.

Once we've paid the fee and everyone has the prints they want, Lysander finally admits, "Okay, Jodie, that wasn't a terrible idea. Although I'm pretty sure we may all need some hand sanitizer. Is it just me, or did that costume smell a little weird?"

"Don't think about it. We'll kill all the germs with a little alcohol," Reed says, leading us to the bar at the end of the boardwalk.

"I don't think it works that way," Avery says, but we follow anyway, Levi grabbing my hand.

"This has been a great night," Levi says, smiling. "Seriously. The most fun I've had."

"Me, too," I admit, not searching for a witty comeback or trying to hide the smile on my face.

We head to the bar and drink a lot of drinks, talking about our adventures, and swearing that maybe we'd do this again sometime soon instead of clubbing.

"Actually, are you guys free sometime this week? Because I'd like to show you all my idea of fun," Levi says.

"Well, we're intrigued," Avery says over her bottle of beer. "I'm sure we can figure out a time for you, Levi."

"Should we be worried?" I ask.

"Of course," Levi responds, before kissing me

passionately. Reed wolf whistles in the background, but at this point, I barely notice.

Chapter Nineteen

Reed, Lysander, Levi, and I head through the doors, a giant cactus sitting inside. Jesse and Avery couldn't make it, with Avery just being hired for a new mural job at a local casino and Jesse apparently having a client from hell.

As we step onto the rustic wooden floor and hear the blaring country music—with what seems to be an extra dose of nasally twang—I start to think maybe Avery and Jesse were the smart ones.

"What is this place?" I ask Levi, who is beaming, taking in the atmosphere.

"It's the country-western version of your club scene. Not quite Texas, but it will have to do. My grandpa told me about it." He pulls me toward a bar area, where men in cowboy hats and crazy mustaches serve bourbon and tequila to other cowboys sitting at the bar.

"Wonder if anyone has some assless chaps," Reed whispers, and I elbow him.

I feel so out of my element. All around, there are cowboy hats and checkered shirts and people doing some kind of line dances that look like they're out of a bad western movie. The place is decorated in saddles and lariats, and there's even a mechanical bull in the corner.

"Y'all look so uncomfortable," a waitress says to us, delivering a tray of drinks to one of the few tables at the corner of the dance floor. I wonder if her accent is real, or if it's simply part of the atmosphere.

"Well, not really our scene. But maybe if you can bring us a round of tequila, it will be," Lysander says, winking.

"Comin' right up," she says, twirling her pigtails and scampering off in her pink boots.

Reed, Lysander, and I are dressed like we're going out to a beach barbecue. "Why didn't you tell us we were coming to a hoedown? I'd have at least worn my boots so I kind of fit in," I whisper to Levi.

He shrugs. "It doesn't matter here. People here won't judge you. Just have fun."

"You know this isn't really Texas," I say skeptically.

"Well, we're not in Kansas anymore, either," Lysander says in his best Wicked Witch voice. A few of the guys at the bar turn and grin. I roll my eyes.

"Oh, hell. Let's just go with it. Who wants to see me give the bull a try? Levi, will you give me some tips?" Reed asks.

"That seems like a terrible idea," I say, smiling. "But, you better believe I'm coming to watch."

Levi actually looks like he wants to stop us, but instead follows us over. The corner is mercifully empty, the bar pretty dead since it's a Wednesday night. Still, as Reed hops on the bull, a few people gather round.

"Oh, this is going to be bad," Reed says, laughing. "But it's going to be fun. I can tell. Start it up, cowboy," he says to Levi.

"Don't you want some tips?" Levi asks.

"Yeah, what you got?"

"Hang on like hell," Levi says.

"That's it?" I ask, grinning.

"There's more to it, but in the one minute I have to teach your friend, that's the best I've got. You ready?"

"Born ready, son. Let's go." Reed gives a pretend lasso as the crowd counts down.

And then, before we know it, Reed is shrieking, the bull not even at full-tilt yet. "Shit," he screams, and we all laugh, Lysander looking more than a little nervous.

He hangs on for dear life in what I don't think looks anything like an actual rodeo cowboy's posture.

As the bull picks up speed and whips violently, Reed continues screaming, his eyes wide. I whip out my phone, take a few pictures. Oh, Avery and Jesse are going to be sad they missed this.

Before I can even hit Send, though, Reed loses his grip and is thrown from the thing. The crowd groans, and Lysander rushes over to see if he's okay.

Reed rolls to his back, and flops a little. I actually start to worry, and some of the bartenders rush over.

Reed slowly, methodically, lifts a thumb and gives us a thumbs-up. The crowd claps, and Lysander gives him a giant smooch. "You're an idiot, you know that?"

"Yeah, but that was awesome. We should get one for at home," he says.

"I don't think so," Lysander replies, yanking him to his feet.

"Anyone else?" Reed asks. "Jodie?"

I eye Levi, wondering if it would bother him, thinking for the first time what it must be like for him to watch us poke fun at the rodeo bull when, in reality, he'd give anything to be back in the saddle for real.

But, seeming to read my mind, he nudges me. "Go for it." His smile looks genuine, so I take a deep breath, pretend to spit on my hands and rub them together, and head over.

"Move over, boys, let me show you how this is done."

The crowd cheers, and Levi steps over to give me his cowboy hat before the bull ride begins. I let out a loud, "Yee-haw."

"It fits this time," Levi shouts, smiling and cheering as I hang on tight, the bull starting its rotations.

I hang on for dear life, terrified about being thrown but also loving the thrill of the challenge.

The crowd counts, and as I fly through the air when I can't hold on any longer, I smile giddily because I've beaten Reed's score.

Levi is over to help me up within seconds. "Are you okay?" His face wears an expression of concern now.

"I'm fine," I giggle. "That was nuts."

"It is a little nuts. But exhilarating, huh?"

"Yeah. Oh man. Did someone get my picture?"

"I did," Lysander says. "We'll get it framed for you."

We head away from the mechanical bull. "Let's go get our drinks now," Lysander says.

"And then let's hit the dance floor. I'm energized!" Reed exclaims.

We head to the table, where the waitress brings us shots of tequila. We drink up before following Levi to the dance floor, the banjo playing a wild number now.

"Teach us how to dance, cowboy," I order, and Levi pulls me by the hand, doing some weird two-step with me. Reed and Lysander crazily dance beside us, making up their own moves as usual. By the end of the night, though, we've learned a little bit of line dancing and had a lot of crazy fun laughing on the dance floor. Reed and Lysander manage to get a cute little old couple out for a night of country music to learn how to twerk, and I almost pee my pants laughing.

"You know, this was fun," I say as we head out the swinging doors and pile into Levi's car. "In fact, it might be my favorite night so far."

"It was fun. Just like Texas?" Reed asks.

"Not quite. But as close as we're going to get here. Which is okay by me," Levi clarifies with a twinkle in his eyes.

As we're passing through the parking lot, though, and heading for Levi's truck, a voice says, "Jodie? Jodie Ellison?"

I turn to see a friend from high school. Shocked, I stop and smile. "Brittany Charter? Is that you? Oh my God, it's been forever!"

We jump into each other's arms, hugging a hug to span the decade or so it's been since we've talked. We exchange the "How are you" and "What are you doing here?" questions, the rest of my crew standing off to the side. Levi stands closest, and Brittany's got a man on her arm.

"Sorry, where are my manners. This is my husband, Allan," she says, and Allan shakes my hand.

"Nice to meet you."

"And who is this fine guy beside you?" she asks.

"Oh, this is Levi Creed. He's my neighbor." I smile, and we continue the small talk until I decide it's time to say goodbye.

As I turn to walk to the car, amazed at seeing an old friend here of all places, I notice Levi's lost his jovial smile and his upbeat mood.

"What's wrong?" I ask. "You okay?"

"Fine, neighbor," he says, as we pile into the car.

I'm taken aback by how upset he seems.

"Levi, I just meant... Well, I didn't think... I don't know. How the hell was I supposed to introduce you?" I ask, frustrated. Reed and Lysander are, for once in their lives, quiet in the extended cab.

"Neighbor is fine, since that's apparently what you were feeling." He clenches his jaw and drives us home.

I'm confused. It was such an amazing night, and now... what happened? I mean, it would hardly be appropriate to introduce him as my boyfriend, right? Because we haven't ironed that out. I mean, yeah, we obviously have something going. We spend a lot of time together—inside and outside the bedroom.

But we're having fun. Levi's made that crucially clear.

"So, that was a blast," Lysander says, trying to salvage the night by easing the mood. Reed wholeheartedly agrees, rambling about bull riding and his technique.

Levi and I stay quiet, mumbling a "yeah" here and there. The tension is thick.

When we get back to our apartments after dropping off Lysander and Reed, I hold my breath at the door, wondering what's going to happen or what I should say.

Do we handle this right here? Do we talk about the whole scene? Or do I let it go?

Levi answers the question for me. He kisses me, a long, slow kiss, and then says, "Good night, *neighbor*," biting into the final word so that it contradicts with the touch of his lips on mine. Then he crosses over to his door and heads into his apartment without looking back.

I stand on the front lawn, looking at the overcast sky, and wonder what is going on. How did we get in this weird state of limbo, and how do we get out of it?

Most of all, is getting out of limbo exactly what we're supposed to do, or are the floodgates to trouble and disappointment going to open up?

I don't know anymore. I don't know a damn thing.

Chapter Twenty

It feels like we're back to square one as I stomp over to Levi's apartment the next morning, my orange flip-flops on my feet. The morning air has a bite, the change from summer to fall hinted at with the crisp feel of it. Change is coming, that's for sure.

I'm wearing leggings and a T-shirt this time around, but I'm certain I'm wearing the same expression as I was the first day I met Levi.

Except this time, I'm about ten times angrier. I pound on the door five times until he wanders over to answer.

"What the hell, Levi?" I demand, waving an envelope crazily in his face.

He rubs the sleep from his eyes. "What is it?" he asks.

I storm past him, shoving my way in. "You know damn well what it is. Why would you do this? What, you think you can just buy me? Like I'm some sort of weird hooker? Sex in exchange for half-price rent, is that what this is?"

I'm seething in anger, the invoice in my mailbox sending me in a fury.

Levi clutches his head. "Jodie, calm down. Jesus. I was trying to help."

I stomp around the living room, trying to think but spewing words instead. "By cutting my rent in half? I didn't ask you to do this."

"I know. I was trying to be nice, help you out. I know you were stressed about the whole roommate thing." His voice registers frustration, but I'm stewing in my own anger.

"That doesn't mean I wanted to be bought." And there it is, the truth behind my anger. He's struck a nerve, one I didn't realize was so sensitive.

I don't want to feel bought. I don't want to feel used.

Even as the words fly out of my mouth, I know they sound crazy. I know I need to reel it back in.

But something about that letter this morning sent me over the edge.

In truth, if I stop and think about it, maybe it's a buildup. It's a buildup of this increasing tension I feel trying to figure out what the hell this is with Levi. Maybe it's because every time I'm around him, "just fun" doesn't fit anymore, not even close.

I'm falling for him, crazy falling for him. And I'm scared. I'm scared that it's a mistake or a disaster in the making. Most of all, I'm scared he doesn't feel the shift. I'm scared he's still in the fun zone, and I'm bound for heartbreak, the worst kind of heartbreak—the one-sided, solitary kind.

So when I got up and found the half-price rent bill this

morning, I exploded.

I, Jodie Ellison, don't need to be saved by a man, especially a man who has vowed to just have fun with me. I don't need a man who will cut my bill in half while I'm sleeping with him. I don't want his pity or his financial backing. I'm not that kind of woman.

"Jodie, relax. I was trying to help you out. And if you think I'm the kind of man to barter for sex, then you don't know me at all, and I don't know you."

"Well, this isn't the kind of thing you do for someone you're just having fun with. This is a whole new level, you know." I'm testing the waters, throwing it out there.

"I don't know why you're worried," he spews. It's the first time I've ever seen a hint of anger on his face, real anger. "We're *just* neighbors. Remember? I'm *just* Levi, who is just your neighbor. No matter we've made love—yes, made love, because it isn't just sex to me, contrary to what you seem to believe. We've danced under the stars and kissed and gone on crazy adventures and all sorts of things. We've had big moments and moments of sharing our hearts. But I'm *just* your neighbor. I'm *just* some guy you live by. Let's not forget that."

I feel tears forming, but my pride kicks in. I won't let him get to me. I toss the letter at him. "You know what, Levi Creed, you can call your grandfather and get him to make this right. I can handle myself. And who knows, maybe Brett still needs a roommate after all."

I almost take it back, almost stop when I see the pain in Levi's eyes. But I don't. Because once I get going, it's hard to come back. I stubbornly stomp out of the living room, out the front door, and over to my apartment, slamming the door so hard that a few pictures shake on the wall and Sebastian jumps.

I slump to the floor, a mess of tears and regrets and confusion. What am I thinking? Why am I feeling so damn crazy?

And what did I just do?

But I can't find the strength to go back over and make things right, because right now, I don't even know what right looks like.

I knew that cowboy was going to be trouble. I knew it from the first day.

What I didn't know, however, what I couldn't know, was that he would be trouble because I would fall so damn far in love with him, I wouldn't be able to figure out what I was supposed to even do about it.

And, as if to pour salt in the wounds, Johnny Cash's "Ring of Fire" starts blasting from the stereo next door, reminding me how bad love does burn.

Chapter Twenty-One

Three days.

That's how many days the music blares and Johnny Cash squawks nonstop.

That's how many days I lock myself in my apartment, calling off sick at Midsummer Nights and ignoring my phone other than a few obligatory texts to Avery and Lysander to tell them I'll be fine, just have a case of the flu.

That's how many days I pour myself into those shoved-aside chapters in my forgotten manuscript, finding that anger and pain are good for the writer's soul. Somehow, even with the noise and the reminder that the cause of my pain is only a paper-thin wall away, I get the manuscript done and submitted.

My editor likes it.

I don't want to celebrate.

On the fourth day, there's a knock at my door, and my heart leaps a little thinking maybe there will be a familiar, clean-shaven face at my door, and I'll fall into his arms like in some sappy movie.

I fling it open, primping my hair, but am met with a

different familiar face.

Avery. She's holding a bag of Chinese takeout and Henry's leash.

"We thought you could use some visitors and some comfort."

"How did you know?" I ask.

"Listen, when you call off sick at Midsummer Nights, there's something wrong. You've only done that a few distinctive times in your life, and they all involved heartbreak."

I usher her in, and she heads straight to the kitchen island. I stoop down to give my favorite dog a hug, and he gives me a huge slurp on the face in return. I hug him for a long moment before heading to the island, the smell of General Tso's chicken luring me forward.

"Spill. What's going on?" Avery asks as she dishes out the food.

"I think I messed up. I don't know."

"What happened? Reed and Lysander said things got awkward after the whole incident with Brittany at Line Dancing in the Sand Bar. Wow, that name's a mouthful," she says, adding the last part as an aside.

"Yeah. And then, well, the next day, I got a bill in the mail for rent. It was half the usual amount."

Avery blinks at me. "I'm not following. How's this a problem?"

"Because it was Levi."

"I see that. But how is this financial saving grace a problem?"

"Because I don't want to feel like his charity case. I don't want to be some hooker."

Avery blinks at me again. "I'm sorry. I really am. But I'm still not following. How the hell does the word 'hooker' make its way into this situation?"

"Because Levi wants to have fun, basically neighbors with benefits. But then, in exchange, he slashes my rent bill in half? Sorry, it makes me feel like a hooker."

Avery laughs. I glare.

"I'm sorry. I'm really trying to be on your side here. But you're mad because you think Levi cutting your rent, which is what you need by the way to solve your dilemma, makes you a hooker? That is the craziest thing."

I sigh. "Okay, at the time it made sense. I don't know. If it isn't like that, then what is it like?"

"He cares about you and wants to take care of you."

"But I don't need taking care of," I argue, digging into the Chinese food and shoveling it in.

"I know. But sometimes it's okay to be taken care of. I'm not saying you have to accept the half-off rent. I am saying I think Levi did it because he cares."

"Then why this 'just fun' thing?"

"I'm sensing this is the real problem. The whole undefined relationship?"

"I don't know. Maybe."

"Then how about you march over there and define it? Tell him how you feel. Jesus, Jodie, what's the worst that could happen?"

"It could all fall apart. Or he could be appalled I'd want

something more. Or I could find out serious doesn't work."

"If that's the worst, then go for it," she says.

"I don't know. I just… I don't know."

I bury my head in my hands, avoiding getting my hair in my Chinese. Avery stands up, walks over, and puts a hand on my shoulder. "I think by not wanting to box in your relationship, you boxed yourselves in. Things change, and Levi's not Darren, you know? Stop being afraid of love. Stop being afraid of commitment. Because, in the end, you might find it's the best thing for you."

"Maybe. We'll see."

"Now, cheer up, eat your Chinese, and then get dressed. We're going shopping."

"Retail therapy?" I grin.

"Learned from the best, didn't I?" she asks, and I smile.

There's nothing like shoe shopping to forget your love life is a freaking disaster.

Chapter Twenty-Two

"Surprise!"

Walking through the door after a shift at Midsummer Nights, I stand stunned in my apartment.

My mother's beaming face in my kitchen, although a joyful sight, is not quite what I was expecting.

After a moment, we run to each other, leaping into each other's arms, squeezing for a long time.

"Oh my God, what are you doing here? I thought you were headed to Spain next?" I ask, pulling back to look at my mom. Her blonde hair has grown even longer since I last saw her, and she's rocking a killer tan. She looks like a supermodel. The traveling lifestyle suits her well.

"I was, but I missed my girl. Thought I'd surprise you and swing by. I've been gone so long, and it's great, but I miss the hell out of you. I'm only here for a day before it's off to the next adventure."

I dump my keys and phone on the counter, grabbing a

seat at the island. I feel emotional, not realizing how much I've missed Mom.

"How'd you get in?" I ask, as she takes a seat across from me.

"That gorgeous neighbor of yours saw me at your door waiting for you and let me in once I told him who I was. Apparently, he got ahold of the landlord to let me in. Wow, he's a real hunk. Please tell me you've been more than neighborly with him," she says, winking.

I shudder. "Mom, dear God, please."

"Oh, come on. We're both adults. And all I have to say is, any daughter of mine better be quite aware that a sexy body like that doesn't move in every day."

I feel myself getting tense. "He's not all that great, you know."

"Do I sense trouble in paradise? So you have slept with him? Give me details. Damn, I'm so out of the loop. Oh, is that a cat?"

I see where I get my motormouth tendencies and attention issues. My mom has always been antsy, flighty, and not able to keep her attention on one thing for more than five seconds.

I decide to go with the latter question. "Yes, Sebastian. He was a stray last summer, and I took him in."

My mom jumps off her stool to stoop down to Sebastian's level, laughing as the cat rubs her hand. "Adorable. Now answer the first part of my questions. What happened with the hunk next door?"

"It's complicated."

Mom snorts. "Aren't they all?"

"We agreed to have fun, you know."

"A good motto, one I've ascribed to myself. Which, by the way, if you're looking for fun, try Europe. Some delicious men over there."

I scowl. "Too much information."

"Don't tell me Ocean City life has turned you into a prude, Jodie Ellison."

"No, but there's something about your mother's sex life that makes one a bit prudish. Anyway, we had fun, we did. But, I don't know, things started to get…."

"You fell in love," Mom says, not even looking up from petting the cat.

I sigh. "Yes. And then, I don't know, this whole messed up whirlwind of anger happened, and then he cut my rent in half and I accused him of treating me like a hooker, and we haven't talked since."

Mom stands up at this. "You did what?"

"I said, it's complicated."

She laughs. "Oh, Jodie. First, if a man is going to drop your rent, what are you thinking? And second, pretty sure in all my years of messed up relationships and fun, I've never had to accuse a sexy cowboy of seeing me as a hooker. That's a new one, Jodie."

"I don't know. It was fun while it lasted, but, well, love never works out anyway."

Mom walks over to me now, putting an arm around me and leaning in.

"Is that what I've taught you?"

I look into my mom's crystal-blue eyes, seeing such a big piece of myself reflected back that it's startling. "What do you mean?"

She hugs me closer. "I know I'm not the best role model for love, especially with your dad leaving when you were so young. And I know I've lived my life a bit on the edge, and I've given you a piece of that wild, flighty spirit. But, Jodie, that doesn't mean love is a joke or not worth it. Love is quite real. It's just different for different people. For me, love has come along at various points in my life, but I've never wanted the settled-in life. Hell, look at me now. I'm fifty and traveling the world solo. But that doesn't mean I don't believe in love or think it's not worth it. If the right man came along, I'm sure even my flighty heart could settle down."

I blink, looking at Mom. "I never realized you were open to love again. You never talked about it."

"And that's my mistake. I should've talked to you about it. I didn't realize how much of an effect I've had on you. I'm sorry for that. But listen to me, and listen hard. There is no right answer to love. But that doesn't mean it's not real. The thing about being wild and free-spirited like we are is that you have to be willing to recognize when someone's worth reexamining your thoughts, your wants in life. Even the wild hearts can be tamed, Jodie, and maybe this guy is the one to settle down with. Maybe not. But you can't let my messed-up relationships and somewhat unconventional life turn you away from a more conventional view, if that's what you want. Love requires courage, it's true. But that doesn't mean it can't be beautiful and worth it."

I feel teary now, a sense of clarity emerging that hasn't been able to break through. Apparently, seeing my mom was exactly what I needed.

"Thanks, Mom," I say, meaning it as I hug her closer.

"So are you going to go snag up that cowboy?"

"Eventually. But how about today we just spend time together? Do some sightseeing a bit? What do you say?"

"I say yee-haw. Let's do it."

"Mom, really?"

She shrugs. "Figure I better get used to the whole cowboy thing. Where's he from?"

"Texas," I admit reluctantly.

"Hell, yes. I've always wanted to go to Texas for a visit."

I sigh.

"You know, after my trip to Spain, I'm thinking of going home for a little while to Salisbury. But, since you're roommate-less right now, maybe dear old Mom could move in?"

I look at her wide-eyed. "I love you, Mom. I do. But I feel like… we'd cramp each other's style, you know?"

"You mean because I'm a party animal?"

"Exactly. I've had enough of that. Hell, you could even give Gemma Rayne a run for her money."

"Gemma Rayne? Was she a stripper?"

I snicker. "As close as one could get. I'll fill you in over manicures and a walk on the boardwalk, what do you say?"

"Sounds great if you add some ice cream and the arcade to it."

I give her a look. "The arcade?"

"Come on, you know I'm a sucker for that crane game. Where's my wild girl at? Live a little. Remember that time we spent ten hours in an arcade so we could save up enough tickets to buy you that ice shaver machine?"

I giggle at the memory. "I remember. Only you, Mom."

"I'll take that as a compliment. I have missed you. In all seriousness, this travel thing is fun, but I am thinking about moving closer. I miss my family."

I hug her. "I miss you, too. I think that would be great."

"Besides, you never know, there might be some nuptials in the future I'll want to be present for."

I grimace. "Don't get ahead of yourself."

"I'm not. But I would not mind calling that fine male specimen my son-in-law. Now, let's go. I have to be at the airport again by seven, so we need to skedaddle. I want to cram in as much as I can before I leave."

"Hey, you're the one asking a million questions."

"Oh, don't think you're off the hook. Hope you're comfortable with the manicurist, because they're going to find out a lot about you and your cowboy catch. I've got so many questions."

"Of course you do," I say, leading her out the door, suddenly feeling a whole hell of a lot better.

But Mom does that for me. She's a bit crazy and she drives me insane sometimes, but she's the only family I've got left, at least by blood. And I'm starting to realize how good it would be to have family around again, people I can truly count on to stay put.

Maybe she's right about Levi Creed. Maybe, just maybe, he's worth the risk, worth the courage, and worth changing my ideals for.

Now, I've just got to find out if he feels the same way.

Chapter Twenty-Three

I drop Mom off at the airport with some teary goodbyes and some real feelings of loss. Driving back home, I feel lonelier than ever.

It's partially because I've missed my mom, but I know that isn't completely it. Mom's been flitting about the globe for years now. In truth, there's much more weighing on my heart tonight.

Levi Creed.

I return to my apartment, shoulders slumped and eyes averted from his door, because I'm not quite ready to trudge over to Levi's and apologize. In truth, I don't know what to say. In truth, I don't know if I'm ready to reveal my whole heart yet.

I'm pondering these heavy thoughts when I almost stomp on something in the rush to get into my apartment. I pause, flip-flop midair, seeing the cornbread displayed in front of my door. Stepping back and stooping down to get a close look, I see the words shakily scrawled into the cornbread in ketchup.

I'm sorry.

They're two words that are sometimes so hard for us to utter, but so revealing. It's the ability to apologize, to want to make amends, that tells us someone cares about us.

And when those two words are written in ketchup on top of an eight-by-eight-inch pan of cornbread sitting at my doorstep, even more weight is clearly added to them.

At least I think so.

I grin, knowing exactly where this came from and realizing I'm not the only one who is hating this distance between us.

It is then that I notice a seashell to the right of the pan. And then, looking beyond it, there's another. And another. Like breadcrumbs, the scalloped little shells form a trail from the cornbread, through Levi's front lawn, down toward the sidewalk.

"Hopefully, this isn't a trap by some serial killer," I say aloud, grinning as I do what any girl would do. I follow the path.

I feel anxious and excited as the seashells lead me down to the sand, in a straight line to a chair sitting by the water's edge. It's almost completely dark now, but by the moon's glow I can make out the figure sitting in the chair. He's wearing a cowboy hat, his feet in the water.

I run toward the chair now, not sure what I'm going to say or what's happening. When he hears me coming, he stands up, hands in his jeans, and turns around, grinning.

He stares at the sand until I'm right in front of him. Then he looks into my eyes.

"You came. I thought you were blowing me off." His deep voice sends a shiver through me. I realize how much I've missed him and how much I've missed that voice.

"No, I just got back. I had to drop my mom off at the airport."

Levi grins now. "I thought you were still mad at me."

"How long have you been out here waiting?" I ask.

"Three hours."

"You waited three hours?"

He shrugs. "In all reality, I did get lost out here. It's a beautiful night. But I also guess a part of me wasn't ready to give up on you, either."

He takes my hands gingerly now. "Jodie, look. I'm sorry. These past days have been hell without you. I realize you're pissed at me, but I really didn't mean to offend you."

I exhale, looking into those brown eyes, realizing how much I missed looking at them. "Levi, I'm the one who is sorry. I'm an idiot. I overreacted. If you haven't noticed, it tends to be one of my many flaws. I have been rightfully accused of being a bit rash sometimes. And, in truth, this whole argument doesn't have anything to do with the rent. It has to do with my heart."

He studies me, pausing for a moment, still holding my hands. "When I was fifteen, I was pretty set on wanting to become a rider. I'd been sneaking to my friend Bill's ranch for years at that point, learning the ins and outs of horse riding. I'd gotten in touch with a few serious cowboys, both amateur and pro. I'd known it was what I wanted, but I was only fifteen. I didn't have a good start. I didn't have real training, and my parents weren't behind it. I'd only ridden tame horses. I needed to learn how to handle myself on the real deal, see if I even had what it takes."

I study him, hanging on every word, but also confused as hell. I'd been getting ready to confess my heart to him, and he's talking about the rodeo. Still, I humor him, listening on, enjoying the way his eyes sparkle at the talk of the rodeo.

"I knew of a family friend who had this wild horse named Wild Pete. Yes, I'm not kidding. That was his name. Wild Pete hadn't been around a lot of people and wasn't ridable by any means. Wild Pete's owner, Steve, didn't really do much work with him. This horse was crazy. So, one night, I got the idea that if I could borrow Wild Pete, get him to my friend Bill's, I could see if I really had what it took. In my mind, if I could handle riding Wild Pete, I could train to be a real bronc rider. It was a moronic idea. But at the time, it made sense."

"That sounds like a terrible idea," I say, grinning, shaking my head. I picture a fifteen-year-old Levi sneaking in to steal an untamed horse.

"We ended up wrangling Wild Pete, getting a saddle and reins on him. By some miracle, we managed to get him out of his stable and were heading toward Bill's ranch, thinking we could make it. Pete's stable was close to Bill's ranch, so we managed to get him over there. Without much thought, I hopped on to see what would happen."

"Are you kidding? You could've been killed!"

"I almost was. I lasted about one second before Pete whipped me off. Somehow, I managed to land exactly right. Not a single injury."

"That's a miracle," I say, shaking my head.

"It was. And because of that, I decided that I'd get back on, so to speak. I decided that no matter how many times I had to fall, I'd get back on and learn. Because even though I had no clue what I was doing, I loved being on that horse. I loved the feeling I got of trying to cling to something so wild, of trying to challenge myself to do the impossible. I was hooked, right then and there."

"So how'd you get Wild Pete back?"

"We didn't. On the way back, he got loose."

"Shit. What did you do?"

"What any fifteen-year-olds would do. We ran away, scared that Steve would kill us if he found out."

"That's terrible."

"It was. Guilt got the best of me. I couldn't stand the thought of Wild Pete being lost and getting hurt because of me. So I told my parents. Got grounded for two months, and Steve threatened to shoot me if I ever stepped foot on his property again. Wild Pete was found. He was always a little tamer after that."

I smile, nodding, but I don't quite understand where this all fits in.

"Jodie, look. The thing I'm trying to say is this. I think love, for us at least, is kind of like Wild Pete. It's this crazy exciting thing we can't get enough of in the moment, but it's also this bucking, wild, untamable force. We've both been thrown off the horse in the past. We didn't get up unscathed. We both swore we'd never get back on the horse, claiming it was more fun to stand by and watch the rodeo, whoop and yell, but not actually put ourselves in harm's way. We thought that'd be enough. But the thing is, it isn't anymore. If I'd let that first fall off Wild Pete stop me, I'd have never done what I did. I had to get back on and fall off time and time again to find what I really loved."

I look up at him, realizing he understands exactly what I'm feeling and exactly what this fight's been about.

"It's just, I'm scared. This scares this shit out of me," I say, squeezing his hands. "We're so different. And I feel like love never works out. These past few days have shown me what it's like to lose you, and I don't think I can handle it."

He kisses my hand now. "This scares me, too. And yeah, there's a chance that we could get hurt. I'm not going to lie and say it won't happen. You never know. Look at me. I got back on the horse and had a great ride—until I got hurt. But that doesn't mean I regret all the moments in between. I'm glad I got back on, because otherwise, I wouldn't have had all those amazing moments of glory in between. I think it's the same for us. Sure, it's scary. No one wants to get tossed off. But I think we should look at this for what it could be to us. We could be so good together. I know we didn't plan on this turning into what it has, but life doesn't always give us what we plan. You can't always control love, and you can't always tame the heart. The thing is, I don't want to. I love you, Jodie Ellison, every piece of you. And I'm ready to let my heart run wild, if you are."

I stare at him a long moment, taking in all his words, his analogies, and just him. He gets it. He's not here promising a smooth ride because, in truth, no one can. Love is this uncontrollable force that sometimes gets the best of us.

Looking into his eyes, though, I see a man who gets it. He understands my fears, but he also understands that what we have between us is worth it.

And I've realized it too.

I don't confess my love to him or make any promises. I don't have to. Studying his face, I know he understands. I simply stand up on my toes, eagerly kissing him, not holding back. I don't try to restrain my feelings or my heart. I let it all run free as the ocean waters whip around our feet.

"I missed you," I whisper against his lips as he picks me up, carrying me through the sand, back toward his apartment.

"I missed you too."

When we get back to his apartment, we make love, days of longing and tension woven into our every move. We've had sex quite a few times, but this time is like a new experience. Gone is the barbed wire around our hearts, and the protective glass. We're both all-in this time, and we both know it.

There's a scariness about that, but there's also a beautiful depth in the vulnerability. There's a new appreciation for each other and for what we are together.

When we're lying in each other's arms, intoxicated by the realization of where our relationship has landed, he turns to me.

"These have been the worst few days of my life. I couldn't stand being a paper-thin wall away from you," he murmurs, kissing my cheek.

"It sucked for me too. Although, in my rage, I managed to channel my anger into my writing and got all the rewrites done. My editor loved it. Said he could feel the depth of my rage and despair in my work," I say.

Levi plays with my hair. "I'm glad. But don't get any ideas that we should break up more often or anything."

"Wouldn't dream of it, cowboy. Now, I'm starving. Let's go get that cornbread and have a snack."

I scooch out of bed, naked, wrapping the sheet around me loosely. I tiptoe to the door, open it cautiously, and peer out into the darkness. Seeing that the coast is clear, I cross the strip of grass to my front door, grab the *I'm sorry* cornbread, and rush back inside.

When I return to the bedroom, Levi's sitting up, the lamp on. "You know, not sure how happy Grandpa would be if he found out my girlfriend is running around the apartment complex naked."

"I had a sheet on," I retort.

He raises an eyebrow.

"What?" I ask.

"I called you my girlfriend, and your only concern was the sheet. We've come a long way."

I pass him the pan of cornbread as I climb into bed beside him, sitting up as well. I raise an eyebrow, mustering up my best southwestern accent. "Well, I reckon I like the sound of it, ya know?"

Levi smiles, kissing me on the cheek. "God, if I'm going to take you to Texas to meet Mama, you're going to have to work on your fake accent."

I tear a piece of cornbread out of the pan, popping it into his mouth. "I reckon your mama will like me just fine. After all, I've done the impossible."

"What's that?" he asks.

"Tamed her reckless son."

He scoffs. "Hardly. Honey, you don't know the first thing about how wild and reckless I really am," he says, tossing the pan to the floor and climbing back on top of me, kissing me roughly.

As he kisses my neck and I feel the heat rising in my blood again, I bite my lip, taking in the scent of his cologne and the feel of him on my body. "I think I'm okay with finding out."

He looks into my face, nose to nose. "I reckon we better get to it."

I grin and succumb to the passion once again.

Chapter Twenty-Four

"Come on. Where are we going?"

"Wow, you're not very good at surprises," I say, readjusting my sunglasses as I check the rearview mirror and switch lanes. I've got on my bikini and coverup and ordered Levi to wear his swimming trunks. The back seat of my car is filled with beach bags, beach chairs, and a cooler with a picnic lunch.

"I don't understand why we're leaving Ocean City to go to the beach," Levi says.

"Who says we're going to the beach?" I ask, turning to him as traffic stops.

"Okay, you need to improve both your lying skills and your subversive techniques, because really?" He motions to the back seat.

"Well, it's still a surprise."

Levi turns up the radio and then reaches to turn it to the country station. I swat his hand away. "I'm driving, and I vote pop music."

He groans. "First you kidnap me bright and early, and now you make me listen to pop music? I'm bailing," he says, pretending to reach for the door handle.

"You wouldn't dare," I say, smiling.

"Don't say the word 'dare' to Levi Creed unless you want him to do it."

I decide not to challenge him and shake my head, switching lanes again.

After twenty minutes, we've finally arrived.

Levi grins. "Assateague? I've heard of this place."

I pay our fees to get into the state park side of things, and we load our arms with bags. "Told you it was a good surprise. I've always wanted to come here, but have never been. Thought it would be a good first experience for both of us."

Levi smiles. "You're something else."

We grab the cooler and our bags, heading to the sands of the state park and claiming a piece of beach as our own. The weather is perfect, and since it's already September, the beaches aren't too full. Tourist season is basically over, so we take sanctuary in the relative privacy of our area.

I'd worried maybe this wasn't a good idea, the whole wild horse scenario too much of a smack in the face. But Levi looks excited, anxiously scanning the beach.

"Look! Jodie, look, right there," he exclaims, ushering me forward. I stop setting up the beach chairs and the blankets to see what he's looking at.

From off in the distance, the wild Assateague horses are

running along the water, coming our way. A few other people stand and shield their eyes from the sun to get a good look at three beautiful brown horses, running free in the surf.

It's nothing short of breathtaking.

As they get closer to us, we stand our ground. They actually stop near us, kicking up water.

"Quick," I say, pulling him to me as we turn around and I extend my arm with my phone, taking a selfie with the wild horses in the background. I get the shot, and it's perfect.

I put the phone down, and we turn to study the wild horses again.

"Damn, I so badly want to go pet one," Levi says.

"Don't you dare, rebel boy. This is my surprise. You're not allowed. They're wild."

"Doesn't scare me. But okay, Miss Rule Follower. I'll stay put."

We stand, staring at the magnificent horses. I'm so glad this worked out. I was so worried we wouldn't be lucky enough to see any up close.

"Have you ever thought of riding again?" I ask, interrupting the silent moment.

Levi shrugs. "Not really. I mean, with my leg and all, just didn't feel like it was a good idea."

"I don't mean you have to go all-in rodeo riding. I just mean horseback riding."

"No, I haven't. I don't know, I guess I'm… nervous."

I smile. I can understand that. I can appreciate that. "Sometimes, though, you've got to risk it, right? Sometimes, when you're busy making plans, life does otherwise. Maybe getting back on a horse is what you need. Or so some wise, sexy cowboy once told me."

Levi turns to me now, leaning down to kiss me.

When we've kissed for longer than is probably appropriate in a public setting, he pulls back and says, "Well, that cowboy is pretty wise and sexy. But I think his riding days are over, you know? Besides, he's got this sexy little writer to keep him happy and occupied."

"Are you seriously happy, though? When you talk about your rodeo days, I see you light up with passion."

He sighs. "I loved what I did."

"Do you love the thought of being the landlord?"

"I mean, it's not my first choice, but you can't always get your first choice."

"But maybe it's not an either-or situation. Maybe you can take over for your grandfather, but still hang on to a piece of your passion, you know?"

He shrugs. "Not really. I mean, I don't know how to find middle ground on this. What would that look like?"

"I don't know," I say honestly, looking at the waves crashing on the beach. "Maybe you'll figure it out, though. I just want you to be happy."

"And I am," he says, giving me a squeeze. "I really, truly am. This place is home now. You're home, Jodie."

I lean my head on his shoulder and we stand, looking for a long time at the waves, at the beautiful view, and at the wild horses sauntering down the beach.

We spend the day lounging on Assateague, eating the packed lunch I made us and reclining in the sunshine. We play in the surf, Levi tackling me to the sand. We just have pure, sheer fun.

The fun is intensified, I've found, by our newfound commitment. I used to think committing and putting a label on us would take away from the fun factor. I've found, though, it's only amplified it.

As we head back to Ocean City later in the day, I think about this crazy life and how a few months ago, I'd have never thought the cowboy and I would be looking into the horizon, together, ready to face life hand in hand.

I'd have never thought love could feel this good and easy.

Most of all, I never would've thought some Texan cowboy with a lot of swagger and a tendency to use the word "reckon" way too much would come and steal my heart.

***

"Another adventure?" I ask a few days later, sitting back in the seat, my coffee in hand.

"Are you complaining?" he asks as we head out of Ocean City yet again.

I pretend to think about it. "No. I think adventuring suits me perfectly fine."

After a twenty-five-minute drive, we're in a secluded area that looks nothing like the beach city I'm used to. It's like we've stepped into the wilderness, nothing but lush greens surrounding us. Levi pulls up to a stable area and puts it in park.

"Where are we?"

"The Maryland Corral."

I squint at him, although he can't see it through my sunglasses. "And?" I ask, prompting him.

He gets out, and I follow.

"And, we're here for a new adventure. Stop asking questions and come on."

I smile, following him through the gate. We're greeted by a brunette who is sporting boots and a cowboy hat. It's like Levi's found a piece of Texas right here.

"Welcome! I'm Cindy. Are you Levi?" she asks, extending a hand toward him. He smiles and shakes her hand.

"Yes, ma'am. This is my girlfriend, Jodie. Thanks for fitting us in this morning even though you didn't have hours."

"Well, can't turn down a real cowboy, that's for sure. Now come on. Let's get you two saddled up."

I turn to Levi in surprise. "Are we…?"

"Yeah, we are," he says as Cindy leads us into the stable area where the horses are.

I grin. "That's awesome. Although, I'm a little nervous."

"Me too," Levi admits, which can't be an easy thing for him. I grab his arm, leaning in on him.

"I thought the other day you said you weren't ready for this," I prod.

He stops, turning to look at me, Cindy still walking ahead. "I wasn't. But that's the thing, Jodie. You make me want to jump right back on the horse. With love, with life, with everything. You make me want to be brave, to do things I didn't think I could. You make me want to be adventurous and to just live it up. So we're here because of you. I'm doing this because of you. It's time we get on that damn horse."

"Yee-haw," I say, smiling as he leans in to kiss me.

"Okay, lovebirds. Are y'all coming?" Cindy asks. I wonder if she's also from another area, or if it's part of the whole bringing the southwest to Ocean City gig. Regardless, it's cute and suits her. We follow, and I feel my cheeks redden a little.

When we get to the horses, Cindy picks out a beautiful white horse for me and a strong-looking brown horse for Levi. Levi helps Cindy get them ready to go as I take a few selfies—I mean, really, it's my first time on an actual horse. I've got to get this on Instagram, right?

"Now, put your foot right here," Cindy says as Levi helps by giving me a hand. The step looks huge, and I start to wonder if this is a terrible idea. I start having images of my horse running free, me clinging to its saddle with my weak arms, clutching on for dear life but falling to the ground. I shake the thought away, try to be brave, and put my foot in the stirrup. It takes some tugging and straining, but I manage to flop onto the saddle.

Apparently, Avery and I need to consider some strength training classes or something. I'll have to remember to talk to her about it, although after beach yoga, I'm pretty sure we'll both be a little hesitant.

Once I'm on the horse, I smile triumphantly. "I did it!" I cheer like a shameless five-year-old. Levi smiles.

"It suits you," he says, in what I imagine is a very Texan way.

And then it's his turn. I'm holding my breath again, a little nervous. What if this is too much? I appreciate this gesture, and I think it says a lot about him. Still, what if this isn't the right time? Or worse, what if he can't get on the horse? This will crush every piece of confidence in him.

I stare, and I think Cindy might be a little apprehensive, too. I'm guessing when Levi set this up, he filled her in a bit. She catches my eye and smiles. I smile back. He's got this. He has to.

He jumps into the stirrup with his good leg, making it look like he's simply climbing a single step in a house. It looks so easy. Before I can even blink, he's swung his other leg around, and he's back on the horse.

His smile is probably bigger than mine. Looking at him, he looks natural. He looks like he's right back where he belongs.

Most of all, he looks happy.

"It suits you," I say to him, and he tips his hat—in what I imagine is also a very Texan way.

"Are you guys good?" Cindy asks.

I turn to her. "Wait, don't you go with us as a tour guide?"

"Usually, yes. But I know this guy knows what he's doing. An experienced cowboy like him can handle a few little trails. Just don't go wandering, okay?" Cindy winks at Levi, and then she heads back to the stable.

It seems a little odd to me, but I don't have time to think about it. Levi's showing me how to get my horse going, so I give her a little kick in the sides and we're off.

After only a few minutes, I understand the allure of horse riding. There's a majestic feel to it, yet there's also this sense of serenity. Being on such a magnificent, powerful creature sends an energy to you.

"I'm sure it's so different than what you're used to," I say, turning to Levi, the sun above us on this gorgeous September day. There's a little bit of a breeze, and there's a bite in the air. However, it's one of those perfect days when the air is chilly enough to make you appreciate the sun rays soaking into your skin.

"Well, considering the goal is to stay on the horse, yeah, it's a little different," he says, smiling. "How about you? What do you think? Could you be a horse rider?"

I nod, taking in the trail ahead. "I think I could. It's peaceful. Quiet. I like it."

"Good," he says, and I eye him.

For the first time, I'm suspicious. The special call to this place, and the fact Cindy left us alone. It's… odd.

My stomach lurches a little bit. The gorgeous day, the white horse, the solitude of the trail. It would be the perfect spot to….

Oh shit. I'm not ready for this. This is too fast; my heart is beating crazily as Levi reaches out for me. "Can we stop for a second?" he asks.

This is it. It's happening.

And I'm so not ready. How the hell do we go from neighbors to friends to lovers to… forever… this fast? It can't be.

But Levi turns his horse so he can look at me.

"Jodie, when I came here, I was lost. It might not have looked like it, but I was. I'd lost my career, the one thing I loved. I'd lost at love too. I was miles from home in a place I didn't think would ever feel right, doing a job I didn't even know if I wanted. And then this crazy girl came knocking at my door screaming about my parrot."

I want to smile, but my stomach is in knots. How could he possibly be wanting to propose this soon? *I'm not ready.* I try to focus on his words, try to keep still.

"You're this fiery redhead who stomped into my life and never left—and I'm so glad. You light me up. You make me want to be even more adventurous, to explore, and to be better. I mean, look at me now, back on the horse, quite literally. I never thought I'd be ready for this. I never thought I'd be ready to open my heart again. And I never thought I'd turn into this cowboy beach bum who started to see Maryland as home. But you did that for me. You've made me want to settle down, just a little bit, and find myself. You've made me want to plant my feet on solid ground while still having a hell of a fun time." He grins that perfect smile.

"And a few days ago, on Assateague, you told me I needed to find a way to pursue my passion, to figure out what that looked like. So, I have something to tell you. And it's a little crazy and probably sooner than you'd expect, but I think I've figured out what I want most of all."

I nod meekly, my mind racing. He's going to ask me to marry him... and I love him. I do. I'm ready to be committed—but not that committed. I'm not ready for an aisle and a white dress. I'm not ready to move so fast, but if I say "no," which I'll have to, it's going to crush him. Shit. Just shit.

"Jodie, I want to know how you'd feel about helping me run this place."

I blink a few times, making sure I've heard him correctly. "Wait, what?"

"I know, I know. It's a lot. I know you're busy with writing and with Midsummer Nights, and I don't want you to quit that. Just, I don't know, maybe when you can. The thing is, I'm not ready to give up my passion for horses, but it has to look a little different now. And you made me realize this."

"I'm so confused still," I say, meaning it. "Wait, are you buying the Maryland Corral? Are you serious?"

"I want to. I came across an ad for it yesterday, so I called Cindy and had a long chat with her. And then I called my grandfather and talked to him. God, I haven't been this excited since I first got on a horse with dreams of rodeo. I could do this, Jodie. I could make this place amazing, bring back horseback riding to my life. I could make this place the best damn horseback riding center in the state. We could do lessons and trail rides and maybe even add some rodeo lessons. I'm even picturing a mini café or something where we could serve some of Lysander's best foods. I have so many ideas, but I don't know if I can do it all alone. Will you help me?"

I look at Levi Creed and I see something new in his eyes. I see a purpose. I see the Levi Creed who was once passionate about rodeo, who knew what he was on this earth for.

I think about it. It's a lot. The place is nice, but it needs work. There would need to be advertising and organizing. But if anyone could do it, it's Levi.

If anyone could do it, it's two crazy people like Levi and me who just go for it, who chase crazy things simply because we can.

And so, perhaps it's because the idea is absurd and outlandish that I look at him with a huge grin and say yes to a very different question than I'd expected.

He leans over smoothly on his horse and gives me a quick kiss. I can't lean too far because, well, I'm not as coordinated on a horse as he is even with a rodeo accident.

"So your grandpa is okay with this?" I ask.

He nods. "Yeah. He's actually said he's been thinking he'd like to stay on as landlord for another year or so. That should give me time to get this place running, and then I can take over. He's even helped me finance the place, said he really thinks this could be awesome. He only had one condition."

"What's that?" I ask.

"He wants me to name one of the horses Earl, after his surname. To keep the family legacy going. And he said it better not be some damn slow horse. It better be a strong, handsome one."

I laugh. "Sounds like your grandpa knows what he wants."

"He does. And there's something else he wants," Levi says.

"What's that?"

"To meet you. He's been driving me crazy for the past two months, actually, wanting to really meet you. Like, as my girlfriend meet you."

"You told him about us months ago?"

Levi shrugged. "Didn't take long for him to figure it out. He said he knew from the get-go you were my type. Said he figured it wouldn't be long. So he wants to meet you. He said maybe go out for dinner? He's been pestering me, but I didn't want to rush things. Didn't want to scare you off."

"I see. You know, Levi Creed, you have wild sex with me multiple times, you tell me you love me, you tell me you want me to help with your business, and then, only then, do you formally introduce me to your family. Some could argue this isn't the epitome of Texan charm."

We start heading down the trail, both of us excited about the future and about the prospects coming our way.

"Oh, honey, you know I'm nothing but charm. That's why this place is going to have all the ladies flocking here, just to see the handsome, charming Texan cowboy."

I roll my eyes. "Yeah, we'll see. When is all this happening, anyway?"

"As soon as we can get the paperwork filed. I told Cindy I needed to get your approval first."

"My approval?" I ask, a little surprised.

"Well, yeah. I knew if anyone would be willing to tell me this wasn't totally crazy, it'd be you. I need you, Jodie. I need you beside me for this."

"For the record, I do think it's a bit crazy. But that's kind of why I love it. So yes, I'll be beside you. All the way. I can't wait to see what this place is going to become."

"Me, too," he says, leading me down the trail to an unknown future… but one that I'm thrilled to know is coming my way with Levi by my side.

Chapter Twenty-Five

"Thank God! It's about time you let me talk to her," Mr. Earl says, taking my hand and kissing it as Levi pulls out a seat for me at the local seafood restaurant. I was a little nervous coming here tonight.

Not that I haven't met Mr. Earl. However, I've never met him as the grandfather of my boyfriend. That takes things up a notch or two.

"Didn't want to scare her away," Levi says, winking at me.

"Boy, if you didn't scare her yet, it's not possible. Which means she's a perfect fit in this crazy family. How are you, darling? He giving you any trouble?" he asks as I put the cloth napkin on my laugh, smiling.

"Not too much."

Mr. Earl coughs. "I'm damn surprised at that. This boy's been nothing but trouble since he was a little one. Did he tell you how he ran away buck naked at three? Clear down the road. The neighbor had to wrangle him. Unbelievable."

"Okay, Grandpa. I think we can leave those stories out," Levi says, flushing. I grin.

"Oh, I don't know. I kind of like hearing them," I say. "Go on."

And he does.

Ronald—he says I'm practically family now, and I need to drop the Mr. Earl gig—tells me about the time Levi ate a worm and the time he caught a rattlesnake with his bare hands. He tells me about Levi's penchant for tossing footballs too close to windows, and his love of Johnny Cash, which started with him.

After three courses of food and a few hours of chatting, I'm hooked. Not only on Levi and his crazy childhood, but on his family. I get the sense from Ronald that the Creed/Earl families are this warm, fun-loving bunch. I want to meet them all.

"So," Ronald says after we've finished dessert. "You gonna marry this boy or what?"

I almost choke on my wine. I wasn't expecting that one. "I'm sorry?" I ask, not sure what to say.

"Grandpa," Levi says.

"Fair question. Just need to know if she thinks you're a keeper."

I smile, weighing my words carefully. "I do think he's a keeper. We're not really in a rush, you know?"

"Oh, hell. You've somehow managed to win her over. Because, son, I've learned if a woman doesn't say 'hell no' to that question right away, then you may as well put the ring on her finger right now. She's a goner."

I feel my cheeks warm, but I also feel okay with it. I like Ronald. He's a straight shooter. I feel like coming from him, the words are sort of a compliment. He can see me with Levi in the long run. He can see me in the family.

Maybe, just maybe, someday I'll be able to see it, too.

"Well, I'm glad he has you to help with this venture. It's a little crazy, but sometimes crazy is what this world needs, you know?"

"I'll drink to that," I say as the waiter refills my wine glass.

"Me too, darling," Ronald says.

"Me three," Levi says, and we all clink glasses.

"Although, I was envisioning some days out in my Speedos on the sand, drinking cocktails in a life of leisurely retirement. But since you got him to settle down with this corral idea, now I've got at least another year of work ahead," Ronald says, shaking his head. "I guess it'll be good though. Can't die when you're too busy to stop and do it, right?"

"I suppose," I agree.

"Besides, if this corral thing is what you want, Levi, I'm all for it. When a man finds something worth planting his feet on the ground for, something that makes him seriously happy, he's gotta grab it at all costs."

Levi turns to face me, looking straight into my eyes. He grins.

"I hear ya, Grandpa. I hear ya."

I hear him, too, as I finish off my wine.

***

When we get home from our dinner date with Levi's grandpa, I'm feeling good. Okay, part of it is the second glass of wine.

But the other part of it is the security of realizing quite a few things. First of all, Levi's staying put in Maryland, and he's found something he loves. Second, Levi's grandpa is awesome and seems to like me.

And third, talking with Levi's grandpa only solidified what I already know.

I'm crazy about Levi Creed, and the feelings only get deeper every day. So, when we get home and he asks if I want to come to his place, I say what I know I need to say.

I say no.

He raises an eyebrow, wondering if something's wrong.

"I've got something I need to do. Okay?"

He nods, gives me a smoldering kiss, and heads to his apartment as I head to the supply area.

I take a deep breath, wondering if this is a wise move, wondering if I'm making a mistake.

It's a little reckless and a whole lot of crazy. More than that, it's a huge, huge risk. Still, looking at the past few months, I've come to realize one thing: sometimes you have to be willing to take the damn risk.

Thus, when I find what I'm looking for, I grab it with two hands and hurry back to my apartment, feeling more certain about this inarguably ridiculous idea than anything in my entire life.

***

I take a deep breath inside my apartment.

"You've got this," I say aloud to myself. I mentally count down from three, and then I do the unthinkable.

I swing the sledgehammer at the wall that separates my living room from Levi's.

It crashes into the plaster above the Adam Levine poster, but it doesn't go the whole way through.

So I do it again. And a third time. I hear Levi swearing, Johnny Cash screaming, and Sebastian meowing from the couch. Everyone's alarmed, but I'm smiling like a lunatic.

This is exactly what I needed to do.

Once the hole is big enough that I can see Levi through it—who is now terrified, mind you, and confused—I stop for a second, wiping the sweat from my forehead.

"Jodie? What the hell?" he asks. "I'm coming over."

"No, wait," I scream, and he halts, turning to look at me through the hole in the plaster. "Here's the thing," I say, talking to him through the hole in the wall.

"When you moved in, I was sure you were trouble. I'd had quite a few broken hearts, and one devastating realization that forever probably wasn't in the cards for me. Ever since I was a little girl, I've had this notion that love doesn't work out, and that by just having fun, you don't get hurt. I've lived the life of one-night stands and crazy times. I've never let myself fall too hard for anyone, and when I did, it ended in disaster. I swore that no matter what, I wouldn't let myself get hurt like that again. Just fun was exactly what I needed. And then, dammit, you came along.

Your open checked shirts and your cowboy boots in the summer months. Your fire ring in the front yard, that damn amazing steak, and your screaming parrot. First you pissed me off. Then you scared me. Then, somewhere in between then and now, you made me see something I haven't ever seen before. You made me see that love is always a risk, but that sometimes that risk is worth it. You made me see that commitment and fun aren't opposites of each other. Most of all, you made me see that maybe love is exactly what I was missing."

"That's sweet, Jodie. I love you. But I'm not following with the sledgehammer and the hole…."

"I've been holding back from you. I've been too scared to go all-in. I finally admitted to myself that you're more than fun, that I'm committed to you, and these past couple of weeks have been like a weight lifted off me. But it's not enough. Sitting with your grandpa tonight, hearing him talk about going after what you're passionate about, it made me realize something. I'm passionate about you and the life we could have together. When we were on those horses, I thought you were going to propose."

"Oh shit, Jodie, I'm sorry, I—"

I shush him. "No, listen. I thought you were going to propose, and I was ready to vomit. I'm not ready for that. Maybe someday. Hopefully someday I'll be ready for that, we'll be ready for that. But not yet. However, there is something I realized tonight I'm ready for. Let's stop going to our separate apartments, our separate lives, when our lives are quickly melding into one. I want to take our two separates and make them one. Let's move in together. Or rather, let's tear down this paper-thin wall that's left between us and go all-in."

Levi smiles. "Are you serious?"

"I mean, there's a sledgehammer in my hand and we're talking through a hole in the wall all Pyramus and Thisbe style."

"All what style?" he asks.

I sigh. "Don't they read the classics in Texas?"

"Well, yeah. But us tough rodeo cowboys had better things to do," he says, grinning.

I shake my head, swinging the sledgehammer again and making the hole bigger. "So are you going to stand there grinning, cowboy, or are you going to help?" I ask, jutting out a hip now and putting a hand on it.

"You know, my grandpa did like you tonight. But after he sees what you've done, I'm not sure he's going to be so crazy about you," Levi says, raising an eyebrow.

I smile and shrug. "Well, some risks are worth taking," I reply.

"I reckon you're right," he says, as he heads for what I hope is a second sledgehammer to obliterate the last wall left between us.

Epilogue

Johnny Cash is singing and squawking to *The Addams Family* theme song in the background as Reed and Lysander rearrange the drink table. Sebastian is napping in the dining area—formerly my apartment's living room—Henry and Jake curled up with him. We've invited a few of the other waiters and waitresses from Midsummer Nights, as well as Cindy from the corral. She's become quite close to us over the past month as we finalized the sale of the corral and got ready to take over. Right now, she's sitting on the couch next to Levi's grandpa, who is dressed like Spider-Man.

It's perfect.

All around, orange and black balloons and skeletons hang in the apartment—our apartment.

"You know, it's a good thing we took down that wall. We've got plenty of room now for our annual Halloween party," Levi whispers in my ear as I'm setting out a tray of graveyard-themed cookies.

"Annual party, huh?"

"I mean, yeah. Isn't this great? All of our friends, Halloween decorations, I love it."

"Well, you two better make this an annual tradition. If you go breaking up, there's going to be quite the damage fee for both of you," Levi's grandpa says, walking up beside us.

I grin. "It was for a good cause, right?"

It's been the running joke, one I'm pretty sure I'll never live down. Avery, Jesse, Lysander, Reed, and Grandpa Ronald all think I'm a little crazy for turning our apartments into one giant living arrangement with a sledgehammer. Still, they seem to be enjoying the extra space—and the fact that Levi and I are living in it together.

In my June Carter costume, I head back to the main kitchen—mine—to get out some of the other appetizers.

"Great party, Jodie," Lysander says, joining me and helping with the trays. "You and the cowboy know how to throw a rocking event."

"You're only saying that because there are plenty of Jell-O shots," I tease.

He shrugs and nods in agreement.

The party keeps going, different spooky tunes prompting dancing and laughing. It's not a Gemma Rayne-style party. Everyone keeps it pretty under control—after all, the landlord is here.

Still, the party's filled with laughter and fun. Lysander busts out his "Thriller" dance moves, and Avery and Jesse have brought an apple bobbing setup that creates a lot of competition between the males at the party. Joseph from

Midsummer Nights ends up winning, to both Levi's and Jesse's anger.

After a few hours of refilling drinks, making my rounds, and eating too many snacks, my own Johnny Cash—Levi, of course—yanks on my hand and pulls me outside for some fresh air.

Outside, the front lawn is decorated with pumpkins we carved together last week. It's been fun creating new traditions and getting to know each other in new ways.

That's not to say it's been easy.

Naturally, there were plenty of issues and obstacles after I'd finished swinging the sledgehammer. There was plenty of drywall dust to clean up and reorganizing of our homes, of our schedules, and of our lives. There were patient corrections of Sebastian when he jumped on Johnny Cash's cage every five minutes, and exasperated looks when Levi left his clothes beside the hamper. There were compromises and adjustments, learning the ins and outs of life together.

Over the past month, we've come to learn that we fit together—but that doesn't mean everything's perfect. Going from just neighbors to just fun to committed hasn't been a breeze. It's been tough work, and there have been plenty of times I thought the boat was going to capsize.

But it hasn't. Because even though we're two crazy rebels, we've got one thing in common: we love each other. The real, true kind of love that makes you want to jump right back on the horse, to take life by the horns, to live it up.

The kind that makes you want to tear down the wall

between you and move in together because you know it's worth the risk.

"The party is going well," Levi says, kissing my neck and giving me chills.

"Yeah, it's been a blast."

"Not as much fun as it'll be when everyone leaves," he whispers in my ear. "I've been waiting to tear that June Carter outfit off you all night."

I turn to kiss him, his hands wandering to my hips. On the front lawn, we kiss like we have so many times.

"Will you two get a room already?" a voice yells as the door flies open.

I turn, still in Levi's arms, to see Avery waving and smiling.

"Already done that," I yell back, and she shakes her head.

"Will you two get back in here? We want to do a drinking game."

"Be right there," I yell, and Avery grins before shutting the door.

I turn to Levi. "You ready to go inside?" I ask.

"Just a minute. I have something to show you," he says, kissing me on the cheek and telling me to stay put. He wanders around to the parking area, and I stand for a moment, looking up at the perfectly clear night sky, studying the stars and thinking about everything that's shifted in the past few months.

A few minutes later, Levi returns, carrying a huge item that's covered in a sheet.

"What's that?" I ask as he comes closer.

"It's the sign for the new business. Our new business."

I smile, seeing the familiar glow in Levi's eyes, the one he gets when he talks about the horse riding venture. It's contagious. His passion makes me feel even more excited about what's to come.

"I didn't know you picked a name," I say, studying him.

"I did. And I hope you like it. I wanted to surprise you. Avery helped out, painted it. You ready?"

I nod, and he pulls off the sheet as I walk to the front of the sign to check it out.

The smile on my face spreads as I see an adorable white-and-blue sign with a rodeo silhouette in the corner. The cowboy's wearing a hat that has a starfish on it, and there is sand underneath the horse's feet.

In the middle is the name that is perfect, that says everything. I look at the sign and I understand exactly what Levi's saying.

Right in the middle are two words: Wild Hearts.

I hug him. "I love it. It's perfect."

"I thought so. Because it took two wild hearts settling down enough to fall in love for this to be possible. I'm serious, Jodie, without you, I wouldn't be chasing this dream. Hell, who knows what I'd be doing."

"Probably still wearing boots and jeans on the sand," I tease.

"Probably. But seriously, this life we're building together has made me see that love doesn't have to be what we thought it was. Love isn't only about the chemistry or the passion, not that we don't have that."

I wink at him, leaning in on his chest. "Do we, now?"

He kisses me on the temple before continuing. "I think we do. But I've come to realize it's about much more than that. It's this, right here, standing on the front lawn of the home we're building, looking at the future. It's standing hand in hand as we venture this crazy life together, planning and dreaming. It's us chasing our dreams together, even if they're very different dreams. I think most of all I've learned that love doesn't have to be a white picket fence or spaghetti on Tuesdays. It can be fun and free. It can be adventure. That's what we have, Jodie Ellison. And I can't wait to chase this adventure and all the others that come our way."

I stand in his arms, staring at the sign, the sound of Halloween music blasting from our home.

I stare at the sign, which is the perfect symbol of who we are together.

A little bit country, a little bit beachy. Two crazy spirits, two separate sets of dreams, but one love of adventure and fun. The home we've built and this business venture are exactly what we need; it's a mix of the best of both of us, which can't possibly be boring.

It took us both a summer to realize what love can be. Now that we've found it, we don't ever want to think about letting it go.

"You ready to go back inside, cowboy?" I ask now, turning to look into those dark eyes I love so much.

"I reckon I am. But only on one condition," he says.

I raise an eyebrow. "What's that?"

"Well, ma'am, I'm going to have to ask that at this party tonight, we adhere to a policy of strictly fun." He grins, and I elbow him in the ribs as we head back through the door, the rest of the partygoers greeting us like we've come back from a month-long trip.

Looking at the faces in our home, seeing all the people who have become family as I cling to the arm of the man I'm building a life with, I realize we've got a new motto these days.

It's certainly still fun and wild. But it's something else too.

As we head to the makeshift dance floor with our friends, I realize that this life we're building, it's become something I could have never imagined I wanted or dreamed of.

Because this life with Levi Creed… it's not just fun.

It's not just wild and crazy.

It's just… everything.

Just everything.

Acknowledgements

First, I would like to thank Becky Johnson and everyone at Hot Tree Publishing. I will never be able to thank you enough for believing in my words, for supporting my dreams, and for helping me get my books into the world. Your dedication to the romance genre and to authors' dreams is something I am so grateful for. Hot Tree Publishing truly isn't a publisher; it is a family. Thank you to everyone who works so hard to shape my stories into books I am proud to have my name on. A special thank-you to Olivia, Justine, Donna, Claire, and everyone else who is part of the publishing process. Thank you to my fellow Hot Tree Publishing authors. I am so honored to call myself a part of the group.

I would also like to thank my parents, Ken and Lori Keagy, for their tireless support of my dreams. You taught me to love books and to chase my dreams.

Thank you to my husband, my comic relief and motivator. You're always there to help me keep my chin up on bad days, and to celebrate on good days. You've never stopped believing in my dreams. Thank you for showing me that real love is beautiful.

Thank you to my friends, family, and coworkers who help me with my writing journey. Thank you especially to Bonnie Keagy, Christie James, Kristin Books, Kristin Mathias, Jamie Lynch, Kelly Rubritz, Alicia Schmouder, Lynette Luke, Jennifer Carney, and Dr. Letcher. Thank you to all my online fans and friends who help spread the word about my works.

Thank you to all the teachers who have inspired me and helped me grow as a writer. A special thanks goes to Mr. Kunkle, Diane Vella, Sue Gunsallus, and all of the professors at Mount Aloysius College.

Thank you to Bradley's Book Outlet, Pages & Light, Book Warehouse, Barnes & Noble in Altoona, and all the other bookstores who have graciously opened their doors to me.

I would like to thank every single book blog and reviewer who has helped me on this journey. I would especially like to thank Tome Tender Book Blog, ItaPixie, Heather Jasinski, Books and Bindings Book Blog, Once Upon a Page, Always Booking, and all the other amazing bloggers who have shared, reviewed, and posted about my works.

A big thanks goes to Kay Shuma for being there for my author journey from the beginning and inspiring me to keep telling my stories.

Thank you to every single reader who took a chance on a small-town girl's books and welcomed my characters into the big world.

Finally, a huge thank-you goes to my best friend, Henry. No matter what is happening on my author journey, I know you are always right there with your beautiful brown eyes, waiting for our next adventure.

About the Author

A high school English teacher, an author, and a fan of anything pink and/or glittery, Lindsay's the English teacher cliché; she loves cats, reading, Shakespeare, and Poe.

She currently lives in her hometown with her husband, Chad (her junior high sweetheart); their cats, Arya, Amelia, Alice, and Bob; and their Mastiff, Henry.

Lindsay's goal with her writing is to show the power of love and the beauty of life while also instilling a true sense of realism in her work. Some reviewers have noted that her books are not the "typical romance." With her novels coming from a place of honesty, Lindsay examines the difficult questions, looks at the tough emotions, and paints the pictures that are sometimes difficult to look at. She wants her fiction to resonate with readers as realistic, poetic, and powerful. Lindsay wants women readers to be able to say, "I see myself in that novel." She wants to speak to the modern woman's experience while also bringing a twist of something new and exciting. Her aim is for readers to say, "That could happen," or "I feel like the characters are real." That's how she knows she's done her job.

Lindsay's hope is that by becoming a published author, she can inspire some of her students and other aspiring writers to pursue their own passions. She wants them to see that any dream can be attained and publishing a novel isn't out of the realm of possibility.

Lindsay loves connecting with readers. She'd love for you to reach out to her.

Website: www.lindsaydetwiler.com/
Twitter: www.twitter.com/lindsaydetwiler
Instagram: www.instagram.com/lindsayanndetwiler
Facebook: www.facebook.com/lindsayanndetwiler
Newsletter: http://bit.ly/2u42BjU

About the Publisher

Hot Tree Publishing opened its doors in 2015 with an aspiration to bring quality fiction to the world of readers. With the initial focus on romance and a wide spread of romance sub-genres, they envision opening up to alternative genres in the near future.

Firmly seated in the industry as a leading editing provider to independent authors and small publishing houses, Hot Tree Publishing is the sister company to Hot Tree Editing, founded in 2012. Having established in-house editing and promotions, plus having a well-respected market presence, Hot Tree Publishing endeavors to be a leader in bringing quality stories to the world of readers.

Interested in discovering more amazing reads brought to you by Hot Tree Publishing? Head over to the website for inspiration:

WWW.HOTTREEPUBLISHING.COM